"If you insist upon allying yourself to that fool you will have one memory to keep by you in the future."

Amanda was afraid and demanded, "Unhand me," as he pulled her even closer toward him, but then, when his lips claimed hers, she could no longer utter any sound nor did she want to. After that initial protest she didn't even struggle. When he relinquished his grip on her wrists his arms encircled her waist, holding her prisoner to his passion. Amanda had no notion how long they stood clasped in each other's arms for it was no longer a matter of the marquess forcing her into submission. She gladly melted into his embrace, marveling at the emotion liberated in her by so bruising a kiss.

Also by Rachelle Edwards
Published by Fawcett Books:

FORTUNE'S DAUGHTER
THE MARRIAGE BARGAIN
THE SCOUNDREL'S DAUGHTER
DANGEROUS DANDY
AN UNEQUAL MATCH
REGENCY MASQUERADE
THE RANSOME INHERITANCE
LADY OF QUALITY
RUNAWAY BRIDE
SWEET HOYDEN

LUCIFER'S LADY

Rachelle Edwards

FAWCETT CREST • NEW YORK

A Fawcett Crest Book
Published by Ballantine Books
Copyright © 1988 by Claire Tremaine

ISBN 0-449-21642-X

This edition published by arrangement with Robert Hale Ltd.

Manufactured in the United States of America

First Ballantine Books Edition: January 1989

PROLOGUE

It was a cold November day. Thin ribbons of
mist were curling in from the Thames almost
obscuring the mansions which lined the Strand
and overlooked the river. Ladies of the *beau
monde* when they ventured outdoors were en-
veloped in fur-lined pelisses and cloaks. Their
menfolk ventured forth clad in caped great-
coats, rubbing their gloved hands against the
chill of the day. Despite the unpleasant
weather, carriages of all kinds thronged the
streets, gentlemen in pursuit of their pleasures, ladies going about their social business,
while beggars and pedlars in their thin rags
persisted in accosting those on foot.

One carriage, a rather old-fashioned, cum-
bersome affair, made its ways from Bloomsbury Square in the direction of the Inns of
Court. The hooves of the team were muffled
slightly by the mist, their bridles adorned by
black ribbons. When it came to halt outside
one of the chambers four people alighted; two
adults and two children, all of them clad in
deepest black.

One of the children, a girl, struggled against the woman's restraining hand, declaring in clear tones, "I will not go in. You cannot make me."

"You must," the gentleman replied, "and I entreat you to recall, for once, that you are the daughter of a gentleman. Let us have none of your ill-mannered ways today."

"And also remember, Amanda," the lady added as they walked into the building, "you will not be required to say one word while we are here. Pray, for once, mind your tongue. We must all endeavor to retain our dignity however difficult it may be."

Ebenezer Dysart, solicitor at law, had many clients in the ranks of the *ton*, but on this particular occasion he felt distinctly uneasy about receiving Sir Giles Devine and when the clerk announced the arrival of his visitors he jumped to his feet and hurried forward to greet them.

"Sir Giles—Lady Devine," he beamed, bowing low before the two adults.

"Mr. Dysart," Sir Giles responded curtly, removing his hat. "You are acquainted with my niece and nephew, I believe."

Mr. Dysart immediately transferred his attention to the children, a boy and a girl. "Indeed I am. Sir Cedric and Miss Westwood. My sympathies to you all. Sir Nigel's death is a grievous loss."

"Thank you, thank you," Sir Giles replied as Mr. Dysart ushered them all to chairs near the fire before returning to his desk which was littered with parchments and dusty old books

2

which caused Miss Amanda Westwood to wrinkle her nose.

The children, some eleven and twelve years respectively, appeared even younger than that dressed in their mourning clothes. Sir Cedric, the younger of the two, sat with his hands resting on the arms of the chair, his eyes downcast. The girl, fair-haired and blue-eyed, stared defiantly ahead as Mr. Dysart cleared his throat and shuffled his papers.

"Sir Nigel Westwood was an honoured client of mine for many years," he intoned. "His death is a sad blow to all who knew him." He paused for a moment during which Lady Devine dabbed at her eyes.

"Yes, indeed," Sir Giles replied in a sonorous voice. "It is a most regrettable situation. Let us proceed so that we may be done with the wretched business once and for all."

"Sir Nigel's will—ahem—drawn up some years ago, leaves all monies and properties to his only son, Sir Cedric, with a provision for a substantial portion to be set aside for Miss Amanda Westwood. You, their uncle, Sir Nigel, were appointed trustee along with myself until both children attained their majorities. . . ."

The boy began to cry, softly, prompting his uncle to snap, "Be a man, Cedric."

The boy bravely attempted to stem his tears and his sister handed him a lace-edged handkerchief and although her eyes were unnaturally bright she remained dry-eyed herself.

Ebenezer Dysart glanced at his pocketwatch, his hand shaking slightly as he put it away again. "As I was saying Sir Nigel's will is clear enough, but as you know matters are ... er ... not so simple to execute. The circumstances ..."

There came a knock at the door. The lawyer's clerk came in and Mr. Dysart jumped to his feet, straightening his wig and pulling at his brocade waistcoat. Sir Giles jumped to his feet also and his wife looked nervously towards the door.

"The Marquis of Glendarvon has arrived, sir," the clerk announced.

"Well, show him in," the lawyer urged, glancing nervously at Sir Giles.

The clerk stood to one side. Lady Devine gasped beneath her veil. Sir Gile's face took on a deeper hue. Sir Cedric Westwood fidgeted with his sister's handkerchief and Miss Amanda Westwood continued to look defiantly away from the door.

The clerk bowed low as the Marquis of Glendarvon strode into the room. Tall and slim and dressed in the height of fashion as decreed by Beau Brummel, he paused in the doorway and stared haughtily around him. He was a man evidently accustomed to causing some commotion wherever he appeared. Wearing a blue coat with brass buttons, wrinkle-free breeches and hessian boots which sported a mirror-like shine, he was the epitome of the man-about-town. His hooded eyes surveyed the room before him, his black hair curled *à la Brutus*, and his snowy-white neckcloth tied to perfection. His appearance and manner immediately proclaimed him a Corinthian and his sophistica-

4

tion tended to obscure the fact that he was scarcely out of his teens.

"My lord." Mr. Dysart bowed low. "Pray enter and be seated. We are all anxious to conclude the business in hand."

The marquis sauntered across the room and after pausing to bow briefly to the others seated himself in the most prominent chair, which had been left vacant as if in wait for him. Somewhat reluctantly Sir Giles sat down again as he did the lawyer who was obliged to clear his throat once more before continuing.

"Before your arrival, my lord, I had been explaining to Sir Giles and Lady Devine the contents of Sir Nigel Westwood's will, as Sir Giles is one of the trustees of the estate."

Lord Glendarvon looked at the lawyer with no real interest. "How does this concern me, sir?" His tone displayed a most fashionable boredom.

"I . . . er . . . deemed it appropriate in the . . . er . . . circumstances, that you and Sir Giles should meet, albeit briefly. . . ."

"I trust that it will indeed be brief, sir. I have an engagement in precisely five and twenty minutes."

"You ruined my brother-in-law," Sir Giles protested. "You are entitled to spare us a few minutes of your time, if only that his children may see the man who has brought disgrace upon them."

"Sir Giles, if you please," the lawyer protested.

The marquis raised one languid hand. "Sir Giles, much as I regret the circumstances

5

which bring us here today, I must insist upon your knowing Sir Nigel was such a reckless gamester he needed no assistance in his eventual ruination."

Lady Devine began to weep softly as did the young Sir Cedric. The marquis appeared unmoved by their tears.

"You lie! He could not lose so much by fair means. His entire fortune; Cedric's birthright!"

All those present turned to stare at Miss Amanda Westwood whose eyes blazed with fury as she lashed out at the marquis with her tongue.

"You impudent baggage!" her aunt gasped. "Beg Lord Glendarvon's pardon immediately!"

Miss Westwood's lips clamped together in a thin, stubborn line, all too often seen by members of her family and their servants, but she was, after all, spared the humiliation of having to apologise.

"It is of no matter," the marquis conceded. "Miss Westwood's anger is to be expected, indeed warranted. It is not surprising I am the object of her wrath; she cannot, after all, vent her spleen on Sir Nigel, who is the real culprit." He looked at her and as Amanda's furious gaze met his fashionable languor he said, "My dear child, I have called men out for less. If it were not for your gender and youth you would certainly meet me over such a scurrilous accusation."

"If only I were a man you may be sure I would draw your cork," she responded.

6

To her surprise and further chagrin he threw back his head and laughed. "Indeed, were you a man I believe I would have just cause to quake in my boots."

"Enough of this!" Sir Giles demanded. "Amanda, hold your tongue!" His niece sank back into her seat, a scowl marring her otherwise fair features.

"Your niece, sir, is a veritable firebrand in the making," the marquis remarked, looking amused rather than angered which did nothing to cool Amanda's choler. "Let us not delay any longer, Mr. Dysart."

"Ah yes. Sir Giles, it appears that Lord Glandarvon has genuine claim to all monies, properties and valuables which were owned by the late Sir Nigel Westwood, by reason of several bona fide vouchers in his lordship's possession. I trust we are all agreed upon the validity of his claim."

As Mr. Dysart looked about the room Sir Giles drew a deep sigh before he nodded grimly.

"Then," Mr. Dysart continued, "there appears to be nothing more to add. Sir Nigel died penniless and has nought to bequeath his beneficiaries."

"I should like to say something more before we adjourn the meeting," the marquis murmured and immediately claimed everyone's attention. "It would be appropriate for all Sir Nigel's personal possessions and those which used to belong to his late wife to be held for his children until they come of age. Moreover, as I understand Sir Cedric is at present at Eton I would like to set aside sufficient funds from the estate for him to continue there until his education is complete."

Sir Cedric gazed in awe at his new benefactor as Giles remarked, "That is uncommon generous of you, my lord."

" 'Tis a trifle," the marquis responded, taking a pinch of snuff from a jewelled box he'd removed from his pocket.

"Oh, you cannot think to accept his charity," Amanda cried, looking from her uncle to her brother.

"Be silent, child!" her uncle cried, and Cedric said in a soft voice, "Hush, Amanda, do."

The marquis got to his feet. "Sir Giles, Lady Devine," he said, bowing to them briefly.

Sir Giles and Mr. Dysart rose too and when Lord Glendarvon got half-way across the room he paused in front of Amanda. He could not mistake the look she addressed him. It was one of pure hatred.

"How is Miss Westwood being educated?" he asked.

"By a governess," Lady Devine replied. "At least she was until very recently. She may, in future, be obliged to share my own daughter's governess although Miss Cooper has enough in hand attending our own children."

After lengthy scrutiny and some evident thought the marquis at last drew his gaze away from the girl to look at the others. "I would be willing to provide the means for Miss Westwood to attend an educational establishment." As Amanda gasped her aunt and uncle looked momentarily startled before they exchanged excited glances. "The chit is evidently in dire need of the kind of strict supervision provided at such an establishment, which, it would appear, she has not been receiving at home."

"How dare you say such a thing!" Amanda countered. "I shall accept nothing from you."

"My lord," Sir Giles spluttered, "that really would be a most generous gesture, especially in view of the child's ingratitude. The chit has indeed been indulged beyond what is normal. . . ."

"That is patently obvious. With your agreement I will ask my step-mama to find a suitable place for her."

He cast her a look which left her in no doubt the kind of establishment in which he intended to incarcerate her.

"No!" Amanda cried, and when it seemed no one was heeding her protests she jumped to her feet and aimed a kick at the marquis's shins. His highly-polished hessian boots took the brunt of her attack and although she did not expect to hurt him the look of surprise on his face served to mollify her injured feelings for a short time. Her aunt dashed across the room and pulled her well away from the marquis who was examining the mark she had left on his boots.

"I cannot beg your pardon more heartily, Lord Glendarvon," Lady Devine said.

"A firebrand indeed," the marquis remarked with no further loss to his aplomb. "I am more than ever persuaded that Miss Westwood should be taught the rudiments of civilized behaviour. Good day to you all."

The others watched his departure and then Lady Devine turned on her niece. "What disgraceful behaviour. I have never been more ashamed."

"I will accept nothing from him."

"You will do as you are bid, and what is more you will go to bed without your supper tonight, child."

"Oh, fie, I am used to that, and even if I were to starve to death it would be worth it," Amanda retorted, exhibiting not a jot of remorse. "Lord Glendarvon is a devil."

"And you are past praying for, you ingrate."

"Now do not get into a pucker, m'dear," Sir Giles murmured.

"The way this child is behaving, Lord Glendarvon may well rescind his offer, and then where will we be?"

"I hope he does," Amanda insisted.

"Lord Glendarvon is not so bad as we supposed," her brother murmured. "He has made sure I shall be able to continue at Eton and that is splendid news to me."

"Cedric," Amanda hissed. "You cannot know what you are saying. That man ruined our father. Have you no compunction about receiving his charity?"

"Father must have been a complete bufflehead to lose so much at cards."

"Come, children," Lady Devine said hurriedly, ushering them towards the door. "Good day to you, Mr. Dysart."

The lawyer bowed and looked relieved to be

over the awkward business. "I am always at your service, ma'am."

Their carriage awaited them outside the solicitor's chambers. Lord Glendarvon's shiny curricle, complete with escutcheon on the door, also stood outside the chambers. To Amanda the coat of arms looked suspiciously like a black cat which seemed eminently suited to his diabolical behaviour. When she saw him about to climb onto the box of his curricle in his many-caped driving coat and beaver hat, Lady Devine held onto Amanda even more tightly, determined that there would be no more unseemly behaviour. The marquis took the ribbons from his tiger, nodded briefly to the others before whipping his team into movement and driving off at a spanking pace. As Amanda watched him drive away her face was set into an expression of hatred.

"Come along, Amanda," her uncle urged and she climbed into the carriage at last, following her aunt and brother.

"How remarkably generous he is," Lady Devine remarked as she sank back into the squabs. "I did not think we should fare so well."

"One day I should like a curricle and team like his," Sir Cedric marvelled as he stared out of the window after the departing marquis.

His sister punched at him furiously with her fists. "Be silent! That man is as wicked as Lucifer. I will not have you admiring him."

Once again Lady Devine was obliged to physically restrain her niece from attacking someone. "La! I confess you are beyond our control, Amanda. It is as well you are going to an academy with a strict regime, otherwise I fear what might become of you. Certainly we can no longer deal with your tantrums and temper. You might even influence our own dear Rose, and that would never do."

"Mayhap such an establishment will be preferable to your grudging charity," the girl replied, not at all repentant. "There I shall not be obliged to see Lord Glendarvon. Indeed, I hope never to see any of you ever again!"

ONE

The bell-like sound of spinet music floated
through the elegant rooms and long corridors
of Miss Millbeck's Academy for Young Ladies.
Late afternoon sunshine filtered through the
trees dappling the mellow bricks of the Queen
Anne mansion, pushing its way through the
small-paned windows and splashing across the
ballroom floor where a dozen young ladies were
dancing to the sound of the spinet.

The instrument's player occasionally called
out instructions to them as they danced. "Do
straighten you back, Miss Moresby. Lift your
arm a trifle higher, Miss Wheeler. That is very
nice indeed, Lady Adeline. You are all improv-
ing but not quite correct as yet, ladies."

As the dance came to an end the young lady
at the spinet, not much older than the pupils
she instructed, turned to look at them. "That
was at least tolerable. We shall try again tomorrow and aim for perfection, but for now let
us attempt the gavotte."

"Why not let us dance the waltz, Miss Westwood?" one of the girls asked, grinning mischievously.

Amanda Westwood looked shocked as was the girl's intention. "My dear, if we were ever to sanction such a thing, I am persuaded Miss Millbeck would have an attack of the vapours, and quite rightly too."

"Mama wrote to tell me Lady Jersey danced the waltz at Almacks the other evening."

Amanda smiled. "Miss Cruickshank, that may well be, and when you attend Almacks, as I do not doubt you will, you may also dance the waltz, but never, ever at Miss Millbeck's Academy."

The girls giggled as they took up their places for the gavotte, but before Amanda could begin to play again they were interrupted by a mousy creature in a lace cap and outmoded gown.

"Miss Westwood," she whispered, her tone reverant, "Miss Millbeck wishes to speak with you in her drawing-room."

The younger woman looked startled, but immediately began to rise from the stool. Her place was taken by the other woman and as Amanda hurried from the ballroom she could hear the sound of the spinet and Miss Murchison's strident tones addressing her pupils.

As she sped along the corridor towards the principal's drawing-room, Amanda's mind was in a whirl, for it was rare that Miss Millbeck received anyone other than parents in her drawing-room. Interviews were normally conducted in her study and Amanda couldn't help but be curious as to why she had been summoned. In the years she had been at the academy she had come to look upon it as home, rarely returning to her uncle's house in Bloomsbury even when the academic year was over.

That was no hardship for Amanda who, after her initial rebelliousness had been curbed, began to enjoy the strict regime practised by Miss Millbeck and her staff. At first Amanda had been determined to bring shame upon her so-called benefactor by behaving as badly as possible and only after realising that the sole beneficiary of such actions was herself she settled down to benefit from the best education available to a girl.

When her formal education had ended at an age when most of the pupils returned home to make their debut into Society, Amanda was happy to remain at the academy to become a valued member of Miss Millbeck's staff. Amanda could not have been happier. Her aunt and uncle were relieved not to have to provide a home for such a troublesome creature and Amanda herself was saved from being obliged to enter the world of the *beau monde* which she had come to detest so heartily.

When she reached Miss Millbeck's drawing-room Amanda hesitated, knowing full well the principal's attitude towards the neatness of one's appearance so she paused to brush down her gingham gown and to adjust her shawl. She put two slender hands up to her cheeks which felt hot despite the chill of the day. Her fair curls were neatly imprisoned in a chignon

15

at the nape of her neck, and without being aware of it Amanda, over the years, had blossomed into an uncommonly handsome woman. No longer did her face bear continual scowl, her eyes were a clear bright blue without being marred by the old hatred which had clouded them for so long.

Although she had derived the benefit of her education she had been much more content after it had ended and she was no longer indebted to Lord Glendarvon, someone who rarely crossed her thoughts these days. Whenever she did happen to think of him, her dislike remained but the passion had long since died. It was a comforting thought that it was unlikely she would ever clap eyes upon him again.

When she was at last satisfied she looked neat enough to suit Miss Millbeck's exacting standards Amanda tapped lightly on the door and immediately received the summons to enter. Miss Millbeck, a lady of an uncertain age, wearing a lace cap and a cashmere shawl about her shoulders, was ensconced in a high-backed chair, a tea-kettle and delicate Rockingham china cups on the table before her. A wooden screen afforded her some protection from any draughts that might be felt from the window.

"Come along in, Miss Westwood," she invited and her pleasant tone afforded Amanda a measure of relief. "You may pour us a dish of tea." She did so in the way taught at the academy, her interest considerably heightened now, for an invitation to take tea with the principal was never lightly given.

"You wished to have words with me, ma'am," she ventured as she handed the woman her dish of tea. Amanda's tone remained somewhat wary even though it had been several years since Miss Millbeck had found cause to chastise her.

"Yes, indeed I do. Sit down, my dear," and Amanda did so. "I have some news for you which, I am persuaded, you will welcome most heartily."

She was more than ever intrigued. "Indeed, ma'am?"

"I have today received a communication from your aunt, Lady Devine." Amanda's eyes widened, for she was convinced her aunt was glad to forget her existence, a situation which did not sadden her. But then, all at once, she became alarmed. "Nothing is amiss with my brother, is it, Miss Millbeck?"

The principal put up one hand to allay her fears. "Not as far as I am aware. Your aunt writes upon quite a different matter. As you may well know already, your cousin, Miss Rose Devine, is about to make her debut this Season. . . ."

Amanda sipped nervously at her tea, for she had a terrible sense of foreboding. Any communication from her aunt could not possibly bring good news for her. "Oh yes, indeed. She will be of such an age I imagine, although I have not seen her since she was a child."

"Well, my dear, the situation is quite simple; Lady Devine wishes for you to join them in London for the Season."

At this revelation Amanda put her cup down

sharply. "Me? Why on earth does Aunt Ambrosia want me to be there? *I* am not to come out. Lady Devine would not spare the funds for that."

"No mention of that was made to me, but I am persuaded Lady Devine wishes you to assist her in arranging your cousin's come-out. It is perfectly natural that she does. My reports to her over the years have praised your capabilities." Miss Millbeck bestowed upon her a rare smile. "Oh yes, I do recall your difficulties when you first arrived here. You were, I must confess, one of my more challenging ladies, but once we overcame the difficulties you became a model pupil. Would that all my young ladies were as apt as you, Miss Westwood."

The litany of praise scarce reached her ears, for Amanda's mind was in a whirl. Leave the academy? Go to London to mix with those who lived a life she despised? The very notion sent panic rising within her.

At last Amanda glanced at the old lady, displaying none of her fear, for it was taught that to give way to one's emotions was not the behaviour of a lady. "It would be pleasant, I own, but it cannot be for I am unable to leave here, ma'am. I have a function to perform at the academy."

"Just as you will in your aunt's establishment, my dear. A social Season as you have learned here is a very hectic affair. You will be an invaluable help to your aunt in the months to come."

"My place is surely here, Miss Millbeck. The world of the *ton* is nothing to me now."

"My dear girl, do not imagine you will not be missed by the tutors and pupils alike and no one will regret your going more than I, but this request by Lady Devine is not to be dismissed."

A familiar look of resolve came upon Amanda's face. "I cannot, will not, go, ma'am, and that is an end to the matter."

Miss Millbeck looked shocked at being spoken to in such a manner. "I cannot conceive I am hearing correctly. One of *my* girls speaking in such a manner."

In the face of such a reproof Amanda's face grew red. "I do beg your pardon most humbly, ma'am, but I entreat you to see I would by far prefer to remain here."

"As I would wish you to do, but all is arranged. Lady Devine's request cannot be ignored and so a post-chaise will call on the morrow to take you on your journey."

"Tomorrow," Amanda gasped in dismay. "So soon. It is not to be borne."

"Now, now, you know full well my teachings, Miss Westwood. You must subjugate all these selfish feelings for you do have a duty towards your family, my dear."

Despite Miss Millbeck's strong words her tone was not unkind and tears stung Amanda's eyes. "When have they ever felt a duty towards me? Had I been left an heiress they would have cherished me as their own alongside my cousin, Rose, but as I was penniless they were glad enough to in incarcerate me in

19

what might have been a ghastly place. Indeed it was to me at first, used as I was to a father's indulgence and a brother's companionship." Miss Millbeck looked embarrassed and once again Amanda regretted her outburst. "I do beg your pardon once again, ma'am."

"You are understandably in a pucker over this. I will say, Miss Westwood, if after your cousin's Season you wish to return to us, you will be very welcome to do so."

Amanda dabbed at her eyes with a handkerchief embroidered by one of her former pupils. "You may be certain I shall await the day with the utmost impatience."

Miss Millbeck smiled again. "Very well, now that we have resolved this matter you may take the remainder of the day to pack your belongings and to take your leave of everyone. You will be missed I can assure you."

Amanda was already at the door and tears were once again welling up in her eyes. "No more than I will miss you and the academy, ma'am. I shall count the days until I am able to return."

Dusk was fast falling. Miss Murchison fussily ushered a group of young ladies into the house after their daily walk. Sitting in her small room at the top of the house Amanda could hear their laughter and conversation at odds with Miss Murchison's shrill reproaches.

Shadows filled the room, the murky corners were dark but no attempt to light a lamp or a candle had been made. Even the fire in the grate had been allowed to die down, leaving the room chilly.

When the door opened softly Amanda didn't trouble to look up even when she realised her friend, Lucy Brandfoot, had entered the room. Lucy and Amanda had shared a room for two years and during that time had become the very best of friends. Lucy's circumstances were quite different to Amanda's however. Lucy had been obliged to seek a position when her young husband, a cavalry officer, was killed in the early days of the Peninsula campaign. As the daughter of a curate and the widow of a younger son, she had refused to throw herself upon the mercy of her husband's family, instead seeking a situation at the academy. The two young ladies, obliged to share a bedchamber, felt an immediate affinity to one another and for the first time since arriving at the academy Amanda enjoyed having a confidante.

"Amanda, my dear, you did not come in to supper this evening and I was most concerned for you."

"There is no need for you to trouble your head on my account. I was simply not hungry enough to eat."

"Mayhap you feel more like eating now. I have brought you some ham and bread and butter."

As she put the tray on the table Amanda replied. "I do thank you, Lucy, for your concern but I really could not eat a morsel."

When Lucy lit the lamp the room filled with light and all the shadows fled, but then Lucy could see her friend more clearly. "You've been crying," she observed. "Oh, how that grieves me."

All around the room Amanda's boxes were stacked, ready to be transported to London the following day. Apart from one solitary bandbox which contained her sparse wardrobe of clothes all the others contained the books she had accumulated over the years, which Amanda valued above anything else she owned.

Lucy came to sit at her friend's knee. "My dear, you mustn't be sad. A sojourn in London will be most diverting for you."

"No, it will not," Amanda argued, her voice thick with emotion. "My heart is unbearably heavy at the thought of leaving here."

"Everyone is so sad you are going, but it cannot be helped and mayhap you will return soon."

"As soon as may be. This is my home, after all."

"That is true for so many of us," Lucy said with a sigh, "but you of all people really do not belong here, and truth to tell, you never did."

"How can you possibly say so?" Amanda asked in some surprise. "I am very much at home here. I have lived here for almost half my life."

"Very few of us, even the girls, can boast such an illustrious line as yours."

Amanda laughed, although the sound contained more bitterness than joy. "My Papa, dear as he was to me, was a rake and a reckless gamester, always in his cups and dun territory. When I was twelve years old he lost everything he possessed to a man no better than himself." She drew a deep sigh. "Oh, I do not doubt Papa intended and believed he could retrieve the vouchers when the cards and dice favoured him again, but before that could happen he was killed by a buck racing his phaeton in the Strand. Papa was foxed at the time so I dare say no blame could attack to the driver. Papa stumbled beneath the wheels, you see. However, I have always harboured the notion that if he had not been in such despair over the state of his finances he would not have been so careless of his safety."

"What a terrible blow it must have been for you, my dear, but at least you were fortunate in having your fees paid and being able to attend the academy. Lord Glendarvon cannot be such an ogre."

Once again Amanda laughed. "The fact is, Lucy, Lord Glendarvon arranged for me to come here as a kind of punishment. I was supposed to be sent to an academy with a strict regime to cure me of my hoydenish ways."

"It surely has. No one can now accuse you of wanton behaviour."

"Oh indeed not. However I do not believe Miss Millbeck's Academy is really what Lord Glendarvon had in mind for me, although 'tis true he left it to his stepmother to choose the establishment. No doubting it was chosen on entirely erroneous information as to the bleakness of its regime. I never met the dowager Lady Glendarvon and I have often wondered about her, especially in those early years of my stay. Lord

Glendarvon seemed to believe she could choose an establishment equal to my wickedness. Do you suppose she is some ancient harridan who wears patches to cover her pock-marks? In all truth I cannot envisage her ruling her stepson, but I have often wished it was so."

Lucy laughed. "You are too unkind, Amanda. It is most unlike you."

"You did not know me then, Lucy. My wickedness knew no bounds, I am afraid."

"Perchance you will be afforded the opportunity of making Lady Glendarvon's acquaintance while you are in London."

"Oh, I sincerely hope I am not! Nor her disagreeable stepson. When I came here it was in the sincere hope I would never clap eyes upon him again."

"I am beginning to suspect that might be the very reason for your reluctance to return to London," Lucy told her with a knowing grin. "The fear of meeting the most dreadful Lord Glendarvon once again is making you a prisoner."

"Fear!" Amanda cried, sitting forward in her chair and exhibiting some animation at last. "How dramatic you are. I am bound to contradict you, Lucy. I confess I hope never to clap eyes upon him again, but I do not fear him. In any event it is possible he might have contracted an ague and died. His stepmother too."

Lucy was obliged to stifle her laughter with her hand. "Oh you wicked creature to say such a thing."

Amanda looked rueful. "I own that is unlikely, but one can still hope. In any event it is unlike I shall see anyone of consequence. I would be a bufflehead indeed if I did not believe I am going to my aunt's house to be anything other than an unpaid lackey."

"Surely not!"

"Why do you suppose she has never wanted me there before?"

"You always declared your contentment remaining here at Aylsford."

"That is certainly the truth, but I have no doubt about the reason I am asked—no commanded—now. Why has she not demanded my presence before? For years Aunt Ambrosia had a companion of sorts—an impoverished cousin—who died this summer while they all rusticated in Berkshire. My brother wrote to me—one of his rare communications—to tell me so. I do not doubt I am called upon to replace poor Sophia who fetched and carried for Aunt Ambrosia, and was the soul of patience, I am bound to add."

"You will not be, so your aunt may be in for a surprise on that score."

"Indeed," Amanda agreed, looking grim. "I have a notion she will be glad enough to send me back here before too long a time has passed."

"The girls romanticise you, Amanda. Did you know that?"

Amanda's eyes grew wide. "Indeed, I do not. I cannot conceive what you may mean."

"They are wont to weave romantic stories around your circumstances. I have overheard them speaking of you in such terms."

"I cannot conceive why. My circumstances

are not in the least romantic, rather common, I fear."

"I think you are, as always, too modest. You are high born; no one can doubt that. There can be few of your status who are obliged to seek employment and, of course, you are very lovely. Some of the girls know of your family and they have some garbled idea of your history. Together with a secret benefactor, they make much of it."

"Girls have such notions, Lucy. It is of no matter, and allow me to state that the Marquis of Glendarvon is no benefactor. I once kicked him, you know."

Lucy chuckled. "I did not. How famous. Was he injured?"

"I regret to say he was not in the least, except perchance to his pride which was prodigious." When Amanda laughed it was with genuine amusement at last. "My aunt was horrified and Lord Glendarvon's expression was quite wonderful to see. I might not have injured his person but I did mark his hessian boots and he was such a dandy I dare say I caused him considerable vexation. No doubt he has grown stout and brandy-faced like his crony the Prince of Wales."

"I have always imagined him to be old and gouty in those days."

"No, no. He could not have been older than I am now."

"Is he married?"

Amanda frowned. "I am persuaded he was not then. No doubt he is leg-shackled by now. He will have wed a fortune, but I pray Lady

Glendarvon is a bracket-faced harridan who plagues his life."

They both laughed heartily and then Lucy said, "It is good to see you come out of the dismals, my dear."

"We should not laugh at my shameful antics, Lucy. Whatever my feelings towards Lord Glendarvon I should not have behaved in such a hoydenish manner."

"Do you recall writing a novel based upon your memories of him?"

Once again Amanda laughed. "Oh, indeed I do. *The Terrors of Lucifer*. I portrayed him as the complete ogre. The story is totally nosensical, but I do believe the writing of it served to exorcise me of the bitterness I felt towards him."

"When you are in London you should contrive to have it published. Such tales are exceeding popular."

Amanda continued to laugh. "Indeed I will not! My childish ramblings!"

"When I read it I considered it to be every bit as good as *The Castle of Otranto* or *The Mysteries of Udolpho.*"

"If you truly think so, dearest, I shall be glad to leave it with you for your enjoyment after I am gone. Oh, I must have been the most dreadful child. I doubt if I would have the courage to assault anyone now, however much I disliked them, but I do recall that after Mama died Papa indulged us terribly. I am afraid I was rather wild in those days."

"I find it difficult to believe now, but you

must own that Lord Glendarvon did you a service by sending you here."

"Ah, but that was not his intention." Amanda got to her feet at last. "How odd it is. I feel hungry at last. I believe I shall partake of a morsel of food, Lucy." As she went to the table she glanced back. "You must vow to write to me often while I am away. I must be kept abreast of all the news."

"I shall, although there will be little news to impart from here. However, the same cannot be said for you and I shall await impatiently to hear about all those you meet in London."

"Have no doubt, Lucy, I shall endeavour not to go abroad more than is absolutely necessary. The *beau monde* holds no attraction for me after the ruination of Papa."

"If your aunt has any sense at all she will concur with your wishes on that score."

Amanda glanced at her curiously as she nibbled a piece of bread and butter. "I do trust you are correct, but do tell me why you say so."

"I have no notion whether her daughter has a fair contenance or not, but she surely cannot be as well-favoured as you."

Amanda's cheeks grew rather pink. "Oh fie, Lucy, I am a very dowdy creature and Rose will have the very best of silks and satins for her come-out."

"If you had that advantage I am persuaded, Amanda, there would be no one to match you."

Momentarily Amanda allowed her thoughts to dwell upon the fact that if her father had lived and not lost his fortune she too would have had the finest gowns and glittering parties in her come-out year. No doubt she would have been married by now, being possessed of a fair portion. There might even have been a child in the nursery.

Quickly she thrust the discomforting thought from her mind. "Long ago I became resigned to the fact I shall never marry. It would be impossible for me, I think. A man of my station with a title seeks a fortune to supplement his own, and one who is penniless seeks elevation to a more comfortable existence."

Lucy sighed. "It would be difficult, I own, but not, I'm persuaded, impossible for you. My own marriage was a brief one, but I was happy for a while. I would wish that for you too."

Amanda bent down to kiss her. "I am content enough and have the consolation of knowing I shall not become leg-shackled to a rake who is for ever foxed and determined to gamble away his last guinea."

"Not all gentlemen are like that, Amanda."

"Mayhap they are not," she answered thoughtfully and then smiled at her friend. "Our little coze has served to raise my spirits, as always. That is something I shall surely miss when I am in London.'

"So shall I," Lucy mused. "Mayhap it will not be for too long a time."

But she did not sound too hopeful of that.

TWO

Despite the heaviness of her heart, Amanda could not help but peer out of the window of the post-chaise with very great interest when it entered London. It had been so long since her last visit and so used was she to the quiet of the country life around Aylsford she found it difficult to recall how busy the streets of London could be.

As the post-chaise neared her uncle's house, the traffic became more dense. Pavements were thronged with people dressed in the most fashionable clothes mingling with liveried servants who were going about their master's business, and pedlars selling everything from apples to pots and pans. The noise was something she would be obliged to get used to again. The sights and sounds of the city brought back memories of the happy times she spent in London with her parents and brother. Having so recently bade fond farewells to all her friends at Aylsford, Amanda did not wish to dwell on thoughts which could only cast her into a mood of gloom once again.

She drew her gaze away from all the activity outside to dwell upon the number of gifts presented to her on her departure from the academy. Pin cushions, handkerchief bags, pieces of ribbon, a velvet choker, some of the items hastily executed, others which had obviously been prepared for Christmas. Most precious of all was a leather-bound copy of *Childe Harold's Pilgrimage*, handed to her by Lucy as they bade farewell to each other. Amanda's eyes filled with tears as she perused the gifts. She would not exchange any of them for all the jewels belonging to the haughty ladies of the *ton*.

When the post-chaise came to a halt Amanda realised she had reached her destination at last. Her uncle's house looked as splendid as she had expected. There was fresh white paint on the door and windows, the brass knocker and lamps shone in the late afternoon sunshine. All at once her heart was heavy again, for she had never entered her uncle's house without feeling sad, and today was no exception.

As soon as she had climbed down her uncle's footmen began to unload her luggage. With head erect Amanda walked into the hall of Sir Giles Devine's house to be greeted by Grimshawe, the house-steward.

"Welcome back, Miss Westwood," he said and she felt his welcome was a genuine one despite the fact she had plagued all the servants mercilessly in the short time she had stayed there after her father's death.

"Thank you, Grimshawe. I hope you are keeping well. And Mrs. Grimshawe too."

"Yes, I thank you, ma'am."

"Are Sir Giles and Lady Devine at home?" she asked, anxious to have her first meeting with them as soon as possible.

"I regret that Sir Giles and Lady Devine are dining out today, but I have taken the liberty of setting out a cold collation in the dining-room."

"That will be most welcome. I shall eat just as soon as I have washed," she replied, not at all surprised that her aunt and uncle had forebore to leave a message of welcome for her.

When she was shown into her bedchamber all Amanda's earlier suspicions were confirmed, for she was to occupy the late Sophia Bridgeford's room. Amanda recalled the poor, mousy creature very well indeed. A distant and impoverished relation of Sir Giles, poor Sophia had been so grateful for the provision of a home she had been willing to do anything for members of the family. The Devine children plagued her ceaselessly although she never complained. As a child Amanda had been contemptuous of the women, but now she found it in her heart to pity her.

As she slowly explored her new home, Amanda caught sight of herself in the cheval mirror. As she did so she began to remove her bonnet and her hair beneath it was somewhat dishabille. The thought crossed her mind that Miss Millbeck would be horrified if she could see her now. Deftly Amanda began to straighten it into the style she usually wore, but she could do nothing about the curtain of blonde curls which acted as a frame for a heart-shaped face dominated by a pair of china blue eyes.

All at once the gown which had been perfectly adequate in Alysford now looked dowdy. Amanda was fully aware her cousin would have an ample range of the most fashionable clothes. Not that Amanda begrudged Rose that, but she did care that people would pity her, as they had Sophia Bridgeford, and she wanted none of that.

Almost as soon as the house-steward had left a maidservant arrived with a jug of hot water which she poured into the washbasin whilst stealing covert glances at Amanda who wondered what stories had been circulating around the servants' hall. Amanda was aware she would be obliged to be especially pleasant to all the servants in an effort to amend their memories of her.

"You must be a new addition to the household," Amanda said as she turned away from the treacherous mirror.

"I've been here for five years, ma'am," the girl replied.

Amanda smiled with no mirth. "It would appear it is I who is more of a newcomer. What is your name?"

"Jenny, ma'am." She walked across to the door before adding, "If you want anything else just call for me, but I'll be back later to put a brick in the bed."

Amanda smiled more genuinely now and thanked her although she was fully aware in her uncle's house her future would see her closer to the servants' hall than the family quarters.

A few minutes later when she came down the main staircase Amanda could not help but recall her own London home in Mount Street, Mayfair, with its wealth of precious paintings and ancient statuary. For once she allowed herself to ponder on the fate of their country mansion Westwood Hall, fearing it was now used for gatherings of Lord Glendarvon's rackety friends and their unspeakable practices. For the first time in many years she experienced the old feeling of hatred for the marquis. Now she had nowhere to call home, and even worse, nothing for Cedric to pass on to his heirs. She could only hope he contrived to marry an heiress in due course, perhaps a merchant's daughter in search of a title. A penniless aristocrat could do nothing else in an effort to restore his fortune.

A small collation had been set out in the dining-room. Grimshawe hovered around as Amanda made her choice. "A glass of wine, ma'am?"

"Yes, if you please. I beg of you tell Mrs. Grimshawe her cooking is as excellent as I recall. In truth that is the only thing I have missed while I've been away."

"I will tell her, ma'am."

"You may be sure I shall contrive to tell her myself as soon as I have settled in."

Amanda was left alone with her thoughts for only a short time before the house-steward returned. "Sir Cedric is here to see you, ma'am."

Immediately Amanda was on her feet, the plate clattering onto the table. Her brother came hurrying into the room and Amanda could do nothing but stare at him in astonishment. Because she had remained at Aylsford she and Cedric had had no contact apart from sporadic letters in all that time. Now some nineteen years of age and dressed in the height of fashion Amanda could only gaze at him in awe. Their looks and colouring had always been similar, both favouring their mother who had been in her day a great Society beauty. Amanda recalled her brother as a little fair-haired boy to whom she had tearfully bade farewell as he went on his way to Eton College and she to Miss Millbeck's Academy. Cedric had changed immeasurably since then. He had grown tall, out-stripping his sister by at least six inches. His shoulders had broadened to carry his well-cut coat in the perfect manner, and his hair, once unruly, was now curled and pomaded à la Brutus. When he entered the room it was immediately evident by his expression he too was surprised at the change in her.

"Cedric," she gasped and then ran towards him to be clasped in his arms. "Oh, it is so good to see you at last. I have missed you so much."

"And I you, Manda," he said, using his old childhood name for her. Then, holding her at arm's length he studied her carefully for a moment or two before shaking his head. "I cannot credit it is you here at last."

She laughed through the tears which were misting her eyes. "Have I changed so much?"

"For the better, for I am persuaded the hoyden is gone for ever. You have become a beauty, I cannot credit it, even though you are a mite shabby, I am bound to say. Yes, there is not doubt you are a trifle unfashionable, my dear."

"Which cannot be said of you," she responded, not at all put out by his criticism. "How fine you look. You're a bang-up blade, Cedric, a Corinthian, no less. I truly cannot credit it."

Sir Cedric pulled at his buff-coloured waistcoat. "Do you like it? The coat's from Weston, you know. Boots from Hoby," he added, showing them to her. "The Beau himself does no better, I'm told. I declare he cannot tie his neckcloth as well as I."

Amanda nodded wryly. "So it would seem, but how do you afford it, Cedric? You are just finished at Eton and not yet gone up to Cambridge. I cannot conceive how it is possible for you to afford to dress as well as you do."

Sir Cedric walked across to the table where he picked up an apple with which he began to play. "Glendarvon gives me an allowance," he said in a muted tone, unable to look directly at her.

Amanda's eyes opened wide with shock. "Glendarvon! Cedric, how could you? Oh, I truly cannot credit what you have told me. Do say you are gammoning me."

"Manda, you really are a quiz, to get into a pucker over such a trifle."

"You cannot help but be aware of how strongly I feel about that man, so it cannot be deemed a trifle."

"You cannot feel more strongly than I do about being dished up. If I enjoyed being pursued by the duns I'd have more hair than wit." Suddenly his manner softened. "Why do you ride grub over such a trifle, Manda? Glendarvon has sponsored our education so why should I not accept an allowance. It is, after all, *our* fortune."

"No, Cedric, it is not. It is now his fortune. He won it, fair or not I cannot say."

"Glendarvon is no cheat."

"Mayhap he is not. Papa was always so bosky I do not doubt Lord Glendarvon did little more than encourage him to gamble. As for our education, we had little choice but to accept his largess. Uncle Giles gladly took what was offered to be rid of the responsibility, but I have no wish to take Lord Glendarvon's charity for one moment more than absolutely necessary. We must be free of his odious influence."

"I am no basket scrambler, Manda, but I see nothing amiss in accepting what he offers. Dash it all, the fellow is as rich as Croesus. The winning of our father's fortune was a mere bagatelle to one of his wealth."

"That knowledge has always been particularly wounding, I assure you."

Sir Cedric looked a little abashed, "I tell you, Manda, in all honesty poverty holds no attractions for me."

"Nor for me, you may be sure, but at least I

am able to hold up my head and be proud to be independent."

The young man prowled around the room. "Independent, Manda? Do your truly suppose that is what you will be, living here with the Devines, prey to Aunt Ambrosia's peevishness and Cousin Rose's whims? In truth I cannot see that as an independence, so you need not castigate me."

"Where are you living while you are in London?" she asked in a quiet voice. "Do not tell me it is at Glendarvon's house for that will be beyond toleration."

"I am staying at Mount Street."

Her eyes opened wide. "Am I hearing you correctly?"

"You are indeed." Now he looked well-pleased with himself.

"What about Westwood Hall?" she asked in a breathless voice.

"The fate of the Hall has never been mentioned to me, and I have not had cause to raise the matter with his lordship. One day, mayhap, I will."

Amanda sank down into a chair. "Do tell me how is has come about that you are living in Mount Street."

"I am given to understand Glendarvon's house in Tavistock Square was not to his taste, so after he won Mount Street he moved in there whilst a new house in Park Lane was being constructed. Now he has no more use for the house in Mount Street he is allowing me to use it during my stay in Town." After wait-

ing a few moments for her comments he asked,
"Are you not pleased?"

Amanda sighed. "I had long since resigned
myself to the fact all our possessions were lost
to us so it makes no matter to me now. What
does matter is that I see very clearly you are
under his influence. I care very much on that
score."

"Oh, Manda! I am out of all patience with
you. When you meet Glendarvon again you
will see he is not such an ogre. Of course I do
admire him. He has such style and wit. Moreover I have use of his stables which I find more
than a pleasure. His cattle are superb, not to
mention his carriages. Tonight I am driving
the most splendid team of greys and his phaeton. Granted he has a newer one, but this I
assure you is all the crack. You cannot truly
take in dislike a man of such great taste. 'Tis
impossible. I know for I have tried."

"Evidently you cannot have tried hard
enough," she answered dryly. "I found it ex-
ceedingly easy. Do you not recall his overweening arrogance that day at Mr. Dysart's
chambers?"

"Ah but that was an unconscionable time
ago, my dear, and we are no longer the people
we were then."

"I shall never forget it," Amanda resolved
and her brother could not mistake the steely
sound into her voice.

"Time has not mellowed your bitterness and
I can only regret it."

"I have taken him in dislike, Cedric, and
nothing is like to change my mind on that

score. In any event it isn't like I shall meet him during my stay, which I pray will be a brief one. I have no doubt Aunt Ambrosia has brought me to London to take poor Sophia's place as her helpmate."

Sir Cedric began to laugh. "Such a fine independence," he scoffed.

"Scorn me if you will, but be assured I shall not remain a moment longer than I need. Miss Millbeck is holding my place at the academy until I am able to return."

Sir Cedric walked across the room to stare into the leaping flames of the fire. "Is that what you wish for you future, Manda? To spend the rest of your days teaching young ladies to dance or to embroider a sampler, listening to their chattering and inane laughter?"

"It is no worse than losing all I own at the gaming-tables. I am very well content there."

"That is only because you have known nothing else."

"Nor am I likely to, Cedric, so there's an end of it. Do not fret for me, I beg of you, dearest, just because our wishes do not match. We are always very different, you and I."

He raised his head to look at her. "I do not believe we are, nor do I imagine we shall agree on this matter if we talk on it until Domesday."

Amanda smiled. "At last we are agreed upon something. Tell me, dearest, do you look forward to Cambridge?"

Evidently glad of a change of subject Sir Cedric straightened up at last. "Oh yes, it will be the greatest fun, I do not doubt, but my sojourn in Town promises to be diverting too. Moreover, I am resolved to see as much of you as is possible in that time. We should not grow into strangers."

"Indeed not. We have seen far too little of each other in recent years."

He brought out a silver pocket watch which he glanced at briefly before putting it away. "Time marches quickly, my dear sister, and I have an engagement this evening."

"That watch . . . is it . . . can it be Papa's?"

"The very one," the young man answered proudly.

Amanda frowned. "How did you come by that? Surely Lord Glendarvon did not save it for you."

"Do you not recall, my dear? Glendarvon ordered that all Papa's personal possessions should be held for us until we were grown. I believe Uncle Giles has Mama's jewels which will in due course revert to you." His eyes sparkled wickedly. "Of course you will not have occasion to wear them at Miss Millbeck's Academy."

"Mayhap I will present them to your first-born daughter," she retorted.

Sir Cedric laughed merrily. "I fear she will be a long time arriving. A bachelor life holds great attraction for me now."

"As it should," Amanda responded although she added thoughtfully, "but you cannot expect Lord Glendarvon to pay you an allowance for ever. I can see it possible until you come down, but he will not be responsible for your affairs indefinitely.'

The young man bent down to kiss her on the top of her head. "You are, as always, so full of good sense. As soon as I have completed my education be assured I shall seek out an heiress to be my bride—if you have not already chosen one for me by then."

Amanda laughed. "If for no other reason I am delighted to be able to see you here in London. You are correct when you say we must contrive to meet often."

He kissed her cheek as she got up from the chair. "You may be certain that we will. It is cousin Rose's come-out year so there are countless functions where we will be able to meet." He cast her a plaintive look. "You have been deprived of so much, Manda. If only I were considerably older than you I might have been able to do something for you."

Her answering smile was a reassuring one. "If you mean I have been deprived of a come-out be assured I have not missed that at all. My own regrets have been on your account only. You have lost so much more than I."

"Be assured that one day all will be well again with us. I don't know how, but I am optimistic."

"Dear Cedric," she said as they came out into the hall, "tell me where you are going this evening."

"Sir Hedley Flint and I, and a few of our cronies are dining at his house in Brook Street. Then, I dare say, we shall call in at White's or some such place. . . ."

Amanda cast him a sharp look. "Do you gamble at these clubs, Cedric?"

The young man shrugged as he checked the folds of his neckcloth in the mirror. "A few guineas only, Manda."

"That is always a few guineas too much," she told him.

"Now, now, do not become a scold. You are unduly sensitive owing to our circumstances, but recall that I cannot be ruined for I have little to lose."

Although she wasn't fully satisfied by his answer Amanda smiled and she did soften sufficiently to say, "How could we have borne being apart for so long?"

"It was only because we had no choice, but it will not happen again be assured even if we do quarrel whenever we meet." She laughed and he added, "What is important is that we never part brass rags."

The house-steward held out Sir Cedric's caped greatcoat. Amanda was still marvelling that her little brother was now this elegant man-about-town. As he put on his high-crowned beaver and accepted his riding whip from the lackey he turned to his sister once more.

"We shall meet again very soon."

"Yes, very soon," she affirmed. "You look all the crack," she told him to be rewarded by the flush of pleasure on his cheeks.

She watched him climb up onto the box of the high-perch phaeton and just as he was about to drive away he turned to raise his hat to her. Amanda smiled brightly and waved her

43

hand, but as he drove away her smile faded. She walked slowly and thoughtfully back into her uncle's house, wondering why she should feel so troubled when Cedric was obviously in such high spirits.

THREE

There was a good deal of noise in the street
below her window when Amanda finally awoke
the following morning. Despite all her misgivings she had slept surprisingly well and from
the noises in the street outside it was evident
that the morning was fairly well advanced.

During her sojourn at Aylsford, Amanda had
grown accustomed to retiring at a reasonable
hour and rising early on the morrow. In London she recalled that the opposite was true, for
social events continued until very late and rising was delayed until mid-morning or even
later. The journey from Aylsford, however,
must have tired her more than she appreciated so she fell into the late rising routine from
the outset of her stay.

For a short while she remained in her bed,
listening to the pedlars and hawkers calling
out their wares in the street below. The sound
of carriage wheels and horse's hooves was in-
cessant on the road and occasionally she heard
a shrill cry when an accident was only just
averted. Amanda made no attempt to get out

of bed and at last was obliged to recognise her own reluctance to face the family she had parted from on such strained terms. However, the decision was made for her when Jenny arrived with hot water, followed by another maid bearing a cup of chocolate.

After they had gone, Amanda had no choice but to rise. Jenny had carefully unpacked all her belongings the previous evening and now as Amanda surveyed the meagre selection of clothes in the press they appeared particularly dowdy. In the country she had scarcely given her appearance a thought, save to appear neat, but now she was back in Town she couldn't help but wish her wardrobe was more up to date and stylish.

After a while Amanda decided to wear her blue chintz gown which would have to do. In any event there was no one whom she wished to impress.

When she went into the breakfast room a little while later both her aunt and uncle were present as well as her cousin, Rose. Sir Giles and Lady Devine had changed little in the intervening years. The lines of dissatisfaction which had always been etched into the corners of Lady Devine's mouth seemed to have deepened and Sir Gile's face was more florid than Amanda recalled.

However, her cousin had changed considerably since Amanda had last seen her as a ten-year-old child. Always the possessor of a certain prettiness, somehow Rose had not fulfilled her earlier promise and would never be a beauty. Her complexion held an unhealthy pallor and her figure was not full enough for true beauty. Amanda remembered her as her parents' spoiled darling, but as one who had been greatly indulged by a parent herself she did not intend to hold that against her cousin who might well have changed as much as she had since childhood. Rose's dark hair had been arranged into a fashionable array of curls which became her well, and her morning gown was modishly high-waisted and made from Indian cotton.

"It would appear," Sir Giles commented to his wife and daughter who were not listening to him, "Wellington has Boney on the run at last."

His wife looked at him at last. "That is a considerable relief to me. 'Tis to be hoped more officers will be able to return to London. Routs have a serious imbalance of male and female of late."

"Good morning," Amanda greeted them as she paused in the doorway.

All three turned to look at her. Sir Giles was eating a slice of ham whilst perusing the *Morning Post*. Lady Devine had been reading an invitation while Rose had been chattering away despite the fact that neither of her parents were listening to her.

"Well, we heard you had arrived safely," Lady Devine responded. "I trust you had an uneventful journey."

"Yes, I thank you, Aunt Ambrosia."

Sir Giles struggled to his feet, tearing off his linen napkin and throwing down his newspaper. "Amanda, my dear girl, how good it is to

47

see you again. My, how you have grown. You are quite the lady now, is she not, Ambrosia? What a pity we couldn't be here to greet you on your arrival, but long-standing engagements you know." He laughed gruffly as he came to lead her to the table where her aunt and cousin were still staring at her.

As she sat down at the table Amanda smiled at her cousin. "Hello Rose. It is good to see you again after all these years."

The girl looked away. "And you, Amanda. It must be very strange to be here after what you are used to at Aylsford."

"Oh indeed. Aylsford is such a welcoming place." Amanda cast her aunt a smile before helping herself to food while a footman poured coffee for her.

Sir Giles cleared his throat before saying, "I believe I will go now and allow you ladies to chatter while I go about my business. You will have a lot to discuss I do not doubt."

After he had gone Lady Devine commented, returning her attention to her own breakfast, "You still possess a bold spirit, I notice, Amanda."

Although Amanda knew she was being reproved she said, "Thank you, Aunt," before returning her attention to her cousin. "I believe you are about to make your debut, Rose. How exciting that must be for you."

At last the girl smiled and her eyes became bright. "Indeed it is. Mama has arranged my come-out ball. It is to be a most glittering affair, the details of which are still a close-guarded secret." She paused before she asked,

"Do you have a suitable gown, Amanda? Mine is already being made by the seamstress. I've chosen white satin embroidered with . . ."

"I'm persuaded it will be lovely," Amanda told her. "At Aylsford I had no use for ball gowns and I am bound to confess I have none in my possession."

A look of astonishment passed across Rose's face. "I cannot conceive of that. Not even the one?"

Amanda looked amused. "I assure you it is so. You are welcome to inspect my press if you wish."

"I do not believe that will be necessary," Lady Devine interrupted, putting aside the letters and invitations she had been perusing. "We shall find something suitable for you, dear, nearer the time. Before the ball there is so much to be done, invitations to write, gee-gaws to be bought. Sometimes I think it will be the undoing of me for I do not have a strong constitution as you may recall. I am heartily relieved I have only the one daughter and not five as my dear friend Lady Henley. If I had so many daughters to bring out I do not doubt my nerves would be permanently overset. I do miss poor Sophia, you know. She was such a true friend to me, easing my life in every way."

"I was sorry to hear of her demise," Amanda responded truthfully.

"Ah yes," Lady Devine answered with a deep sigh. " 'Tis sad I own, but I am very truly glad you are at least returned to us, Amanda."

Amanda cast her an artless look. "Aunt Ambrosia, how kind of you to say so. I had no notion you harboured such feelings about me."

Lady Devine looked uncomfortable but contrived to answer, "You must know that we all do."

"Had I realised how sorely I was missed nothing would have prevailed upon me to remain at Aylsford all this time."

Her aunt continued to look discomforted but recovered sufficiently to say, "We admired your spirit of independence which is so unusual and nothing would have prompted me to summon you from a life you obviously enjoyed so heartily."

"But you have done so now."

"Naturally, child! You would not wish to miss your cousin's come-out year. I could not in all conscience allow it."

"I'm quite persuaded Rose's debut will be successful with or without my presence. However, now that I am here in Town I hope to be of some small help to you, Aunt, before I return to my position at Aylsford."

Lady Devine was evidently taken aback by Amanda's declaration. "Surely you do not intend to return to that establishment."

"Why ever not?"

"Because your place is here with your family. This is your home. Your poor dear Papa would have wished it."

"I am certain he would," Amanda answered, smiling ironically, and then, "Aunt Ambroisa, I do appreciate it is valid that I am here for the present Season, but there will be no use for me here once Rose is wed."

Rose began to giggle but her mother was outraged. "No use? What a thing to say to me, Amanda. In all truth I do not believe you are cured of your hoydenish ways. Of course I do not doubt Rose will be wed during her come-out year. . . ."

Rose blushed and murmured. "Oh, Mama . . ."

" 'Tis no more than the truth, child. You already have a number of beaux anxious to pay court to you." As Rose's blush grew deeper her mother turned once again to her niece. "I cannot condone your wish to remain as a paid servant of that place. One of your standing should not have a paid situation."

"What exactly is my standing, Aunt?" Amanda asked in astonishment. "I haven't a penny to bless myself with aside from what I have earned at the academy and that, I assure you, is precious little. In the event it would be foolish to act top-lofty while my pockets are to let."

Once again Lady Devine looked uncomfortable. "Your circumstances are unfortunate, I own, but you are Sir Nigel Westwood's daughter and as such you would do well to consider his good name."

"Aunt Ambrosia," Amanda answered with infinite patience. "I assure you I would do nothing to bring shame upon any of you, but do not I pray quote Papa's good name for there was nothing good about it at the time of his death. Had he lived it is like he would have ended up in a debtor's prison."

"If you have no wish to bring shame upon

us all then you will be content to remain beneath this roof."

Amanda sighed softly and acknowledged that now was not the time to pursue the matter. As she sipped at her coffee Lady Devine got to her feet.

"Now that is settled we must address ourselves to the matter in hand. There is so much to be done in so short a time. I cannot delay any longer. Hurry girls, while I order the carriage. We must go to Bond Street and contrive to complete our shopping with no further delay. Amanda, you will come along to help."

"Certainly, Aunt."

The door slammed shut behind her and Rose cast Amanda a curious look. "Did you truly enjoy living at Aylsford?"

"Truly."

"But I often heard Mama say . . ."

She paused and Amanda gave her a curious look. "Yes, Rose, what did Aunt Ambrosia say about Aylsford?"

The girl blushed again. "Well, it was no secret that you were quite a hoyden and the reason Miss Millbeck's Academy was chosen for you was in order to control your behaviour."

"Which it did, but I assure you it was not like Bedlam. We were not clapped in chains and fed on bread and water."

Rose laughed. "Your tongue is still as waspish as it used to be, but in all honesty you are not as I expected you to be."

At this revelation Amanda looked at her with interest. "Do tell what you expected, Rose."

"I recall when you arrived back from the lawyer's office all those years ago you screamed like a lunatic. Papa said you would end up in Bedlam. Everyone thought you had windmills in your head."

"Perchance I did," Amanda replied, hating to be reminded of the behaviour of which she was now so bitterly ashamed.

"The day you left for Aylsford you threw a bedpan out of the window. It almost hit poor Papa on the head as he passed below."

Amanda could not help but laugh at the reminder. "If I recall the incident correctly I believe I did intend to hit him. Only the greatest good fortune ensured that it did not."

"Do you also recall going into the kitchens and throwing cook's flour all around the place?"

"I do," Amanda answered wryly. "It was most regrettable, for cook always displayed the greatest kindness towards me."

"It took days and so many servants to clear it up. I cannot conceive how you dared."

"Nor I, but I must have been the most dreadful child."

"You were. I recall Mama sighing with heart-felt relief when you finally went away."

"I cannot blame her for that. I was a trial to everyone but you need not fear my tantrums any longer."

All at once Rose was serious. "Are you not sorry you didn't have a Season?"

For a moment or two Amanda paused to consider the question before shaking her head slowly. "No, in all truth I am not. It was never possible, you see, so I did not consider it a loss."

"That is truly remarkable, for I would *die* if I couldn't come-out. Mama is buying me such wonderful clothes and it's so gratifying to have gentlemen paying me compliments. Some of them are so handsome, especially the officers in their uniforms."

Amanda eyed her indulgently. "Is there one particular gentleman to whom you are partial?"

Rose's pale cheeks grew pink once again. "*Entre nous*, I find Sir Hedley Flint particularly charming even though he is not an officer. He is wonderfully diverting."

"I have heard speak of that name before," Amanda murmured, frowning slightly. Then her face cleared. "Ah yes, Cedric mentioned him to me. Sir Hedley Flint is, I believe, a crony of his."

"Cedric is such a quiz," Rose said with a laugh. "He has a crowd of rackety cronies who are the greatest fun." She drew a sudden sigh. "Unfortunately Sir Hedley would not be Papa's choice."

"Why not?"

"He's always in dun territory and in need of a fortune when he marries."

"Well, you cannot blame your papa his caution, Rose."

"If I have a fair portion it must be there to attract some gentleman so why should it not be Sir Hedley Flint."

"Your reasoning is unusual, Rose, but it is sound I dare say. I look forward to meeting Sir

Hedley Flint so I may judge his character for myself."

"Do tell, Amanda," her cousin said excitedly. "Do you have a beau?"

"No, I do not."

Rose grinned. "Oh, do not seek to gammon me."

"Opportunities to make acquaintences with gentlemen do not present themselves often at Miss Millbeck's Academy for Ladies," Amanda replied, smiling ironically.

Rose's eyes opened wide. "Have you ever had a beau?"

"No."

At this revelation Rose looked shocked. "I cannot credit this. You are all of twenty. Oh my poor dear, you are an old maid. How dreadful that must be for you."

"I confess I had not thought of myself in such terms," Amanda answered carefully, "but it is no doubt true, and I do not find it in the least dreadful, I assure you."

"Mayhap when we rusticate we may find you a curate or a tutor who will do for you. You are not hag-ridden, you know. There are some who might term you handsome."

Amanda smiled wryly, not doubting her cousin's sincerity. "It is kind of you to think of me, but you mustn't trouble your head on my account. I am quite content, you may be sure."

"Oh, I cannot conceive how that can be. Papa says with my portion there is no limit to the elevated match I can make. I could not bear it to be otherwise."

In an effort to bring the conversation to a

close Amanda glanced at the ormolu clock on the mantel which was just striking the hour. "Rose, I believe we should fetch our outdoor clothes. Your mama is in a fidge to be gone."

At the reminder her cousin got quickly to her feet. "Oh, indeed. How exciting it all is. We have so many geegaws to buy today. However, I do hope it will not be too wearing on Mama's nerves."

"I am certain she will bear it all splendidly," Amanda assured her.

Half-way to the door Rose paused to glance at her cousin. "It is as well you are not to come-out," she declared which caused Amanda to look at her with interest. "Blondes are quite unfashionable now." She tossed her own dark and presumably fashionable curls. "If one wishes to be all the crack, it is imperative to be a brunette this Season!"

Even possessing a knowledge of her aunt's character Amanda had not realised how difficult it would be living with Lady Devine. Obviously she had never before been in a position to appreciate what a demanding woman she could be. There were endless errands to run, shawls, vinaigrettes and fans to fetch, not to mention endless letters and cards to write. All of them seemed beyond the capabilities of her aunt who frequently retired to her day bed whenever she wasn't expected at a card party or rout. He health invariably improved sufficiently to allow her attendance at various assemblies but even that did not necessarily preclude the occasional attack of the vapours.

Throughout her first days in London, Amanda looked forward to receiving a letter from Lucy with news of everyone at Aylsford. Every time mail arrived at the house she anxiously scrutinised it for sight of Lucy's hand. More usually there were invitations for the Devines to attend some function or other. Little gifts of flowers or marchpane had begun to arrive for Rose with cards from her various admirers. Amanda had from time to time caught a glimpse of one or two of them and they seemed most presentable young men. She didn't doubt her cousin would fall in love with the most suitable, according to her parents, and be happily married by the end of the Season, relieving Amanda of any further reason to remain.

Despite missing the countryside she did enjoy seeing the shops again, even though she could afford to buy none of the beautiful goods on sale, and she did look forward to visiting the theatre once the Season was in full swing. Best of all was the easy access to the circulating libraries with their wonderful displays of books. That was one errand Amanda never tired of running for her aunt. She could spend hours browsing around the shelves and was often scolded on her return for taking such an unconscionable time about the task.

When Lucy's letter finally arrived Amanda seized on it delightedly. She had already written pages to her friend, telling of all that was happening in Town, of Cedric, Rose and many of the elevated people of the *beau monde* who were acquainted with her aunt and uncle. Now

Amanda looked forward to hearing news of all those at Aylsford, even though life there tended to be in the main noneventful.

Amanda hurried to her room and broke the seal as she sank down into her chair and began to read. The missive was much as she had expected it to be. Miss Murchison had contracted a chill, the vicar was determinedly courting the very mature Miss Masters, the gardener's dog had been accused of worrying sheep. Amanda smiled as she read, for it was all so evocative of everything she missed, at least it was until she reached the last page.

". . . I am keeping this last piece of news—the most important—until the end of my note because I know, dear Amanda, it will grieve you as deeply as it does me. Miss Millbeck has replaced you with a Miss Smythe. I do not know why she has done so. I begged her for an explanation which she would not give as, indeed, she is not obliged to do. Sufficient to say she appears not to want to do so of her own volition, and I cannot help but suspect there must be more to this matter than I can ascertain. . . ."

Amanda read this last page through several times, experiencing emotions which veered between anger and despair. At last when she put it down she felt drained of all feelings. Tears sprang to her eyes even though she had vowed as a child not to cry even when so many misfortunes afflicted her. This, however, seemed so unfair, although she had a reasonable suspicion where the blame must lie.

After pausing to compose herself, Amanda went downstairs to find her aunt fortunately alone in her drawing-room, resting on a day bed with the curtains drawn against the sun.

When Amanda entered the room Lady Devine raised her head, "Oh, there you are, Amanda; just the person I would wish to see. I have the most dreadful headache. Pray do not delay, fetch me a small dose of laudanum. It must be small, however, for I intend to be at Lady Bridewell's this evening. Well, why do you stand there? Do as I ask; I am in agony."

"Aunt Ambrosia, did you write to Miss Millbeck requesting her to dispense with my services?"

Lady Devine looked shocked. "Indeed I did not. I would not presume to do such a thing."

"I am relieved to hear you say so, but . . ."

"However, I did pen a letter just to inform Miss Millbeck that you did not wish to return to Aylsford since you are come back to your family where you belong."

Once again Amanda became angry. "Oh, Aunt Ambrosia, how could you do such a thing?"

Lady Devine continued to look shocked. "I fail to see why you are in a taking over this. We discussed your future on your very first day here, and it was decided . . ."

"*You* decided, even though you knew full well I intended to return there at the end of this Season. This is not, I assure you, the end of the matter as far as I am concerned. I shall contrive to obtain a post elsewhere and I do not doubt Miss Millbeck will furnish me with the necessary recommendation."

"You really are the most stubborn child I

have ever had the misfortune to encounter," Lady Devine accused as she fell back on her day bed.

"Yes, I probably am," Amanda agreed as she turned on her heel and marched out of the room.

FOUR

Whenever she could escape her aunt and cousin, Amanda retreated to the conservatory to read, in the hope she would not be disturbed. Currently her favourite book was *Sense and Sensibility* which she had already read several times. For the first time in many years Amanda allowed her thoughts to dwell upon her own attempt at literature. Some years earlier, during a quiet summer at Aylsford she had put pen to paper herself, writing a tome she had entitled *The Terrors of Lucifer*, a tract in the Gothic genre currently much in fashion. The villian who torments the innocent heroine with such viciousness was based upon a gentleman she had encountered as a child. The Marquis of Glendarvon. Even though it was some years since she had seen him, she was still able to describe him in minute detail. Sometimes when she had cause to think about her work she was amazed at how much evil she had attributed to the man, although she didn't regret writing it. In any event she did not suppose anyone, apart from Lucy, would ever read it.

"Miss Westwood," Amanda looked up to see one of the footmen approaching through the greenery. Resignedly she closed the book, knowing some errand would be required of her. "Lady Devine cannot find her blue paisley shawl and would have you locate it and bring it to her in the drawing-room as soon as you are able."

Amanda followed the footman out of the conservatory, knowing better than to delay doing her aunt's bidding. The shawl would, no doubt, be in a drawer easily seen, and it was. When she went to the drawing-room to present it to her aunt, Amanda was taken aback to find that Lady Devine was not alone. Rose was playing the spinet and singing an Italian song which Amanda recognised, reckoning her cousin was out of key but she forbore to say so, especially as a visitor was present and she was listening to Rose intently with evident enjoyment. Amanda glanced curiously at the visitor who was dressed modishly in blue velvet with a matching hat adorned with feathers. For some reason Amanda thought that she could not be one of her aunt's usual cronies, although she wasn't sure why that notion occurred to her. As a rule she was discouraged from being present whenever Lady Devine entertained an acquaintance, something about which her niece could not be sorry.

"How long you have taken," Lady Devine hissed as Amanda handed her the shawl. "If I take a chill it will be entirely your fault."

"I came as soon as I was summoned," Amanda replied without troubling to display any true regret.

"What a Banbury Tale. I sent for you hours ago. Where have you been?"

"Looking for your shawl, Aunt."

The visitor, distracted momentarily by Amanda's arrival, glanced at her curiously and Amanda could see that not only was she beautifully dressed, she was extremely handsome too.

When Rose finished her song the visitor applauded genteelly and then turned to Lady Devine. "That was most enjoyable. How proud you must be of your daughter's achievements."

Amanda's aunt simpered. "Indeed I am, my lady. Rose has always been the most delightful daughter. Her nature is of the most amiable as you may have observed for yourself, and as for her talents, they are legion."

Rose came to sit nearer her mother and the visitor then turned her attention upon Amanda again. Lady Devine, noting it, said in a much colder tone of voice, "Allow me to present my niece, Miss Amanda Westwood."

Amanda curtseyed and the lady smiled, turning her handsome appearance into something more breath-taking. "How charming you are, my dear."

"Amanda, this is Lady Glendarvon who honours us with her presence."

Amanda's ready smile froze on her lips. Lady Glendarvon! The name sent a shock through her body. All her dreams and hopes of the marquis being wed to a harridan disappeared in the face of this exquisite creature.

"How do you like London, Miss Westwood?" the marchioness was asking.

"Not as much as I do the country, ma'am," Amanda managed to reply with some degree of equanimity.

The marchioness was not abashed. In a well-modulated voice she replied, "The world, I find, is divided into those of us who like the town and those who prefer to rusticate whenever the opportunity presents itself. Most fortunately there is time enough for both."

"Amanda, have you finished writing the invitations to Rose's ball?" asked Lady Devine, her voice becoming shrill.

Her tone was a danger signal Amanda recognised and she was glad enough for the opportunity to withdraw. Rose was most welcome to every moment of Lady Glendarvon's attention.

"No, Aunt, not as yet."

"And why not, may I ask?"

"There are an unconscionable number of them."

"You know full well I wished them all finished today so I will accept no excuses from you."

"I shall go immediately and complete the task, if I may be excused."

Feeling greatly relieved Amanda retreated towards the door. "And when you have done," Lady Devine added, "pray mend my petticoats as I bade you earlier. That lazy maid of mine cannot do them properly."

"Yes, Aunt Ambrosia."

She paused to curtsey before rushing from the room, closing the door thankfully behind her. Her cheeks felt flushed. It was so unfair that a monster such as Lord Glendarvon should be married to such a beautiful woman. Moreover one to whom Amanda could not help but feel an immediate warmth.

"What a pretty girl," the marchioness mused when Amanda had gone. "I had no notion she would have such a fair countenance."

"Oh, indeed she is tolerable, I dare say."

"Do you not employ servants to perform the tasks your niece is about to do, Lady Devine?"

"Yes, yes indeed," Lady Devine laughed breathlessly, "But I believe it wise to keep Miss Westwood fully occupied for as you know she has a hoydenish nature, and I deem it sensible to make sure she has little time for mischief. If only she was more like dear Rose, how much better it would be, but all the wishing in the world will not make it so. Rose's Season is not yet begun and we are inundated by beaux wishing to pay court to her."

Lady Glendarvon bestowed as smile upon the blushing girl. "No one should be surprised. Miss Devine is most handsome. Is your niece here to stay?"

Lady Devine sighed deeply and clutched at her vinaigrette. "Indeed she is, my lady. Miss Westwood is not the easiest person to have beneath one's roof, but I feel a duty to provide her with a home. She has no one else in the entire world save for us. One must be charitable, my lady, do you not agree with that philosophy?''

"Heartily," came the answer and then the marchioness got to her feet. "Until we meet again, Lady Devine."

Both Lady Devine and her daughter curtseyed deeply. When she had gone Lady Devine sank back into her chair. "How condescending of Lady Glendarvon to call upon us, Rose. How splendid it would be if she takes you up for the Season."

Rose began to chuckle. "Mama, you are the complete turncoat. You have always said she is nothing but an opera dancer."

"She *was*, until she married a marquis. Now it is of no account, for she has so many influential acquaintances. That is what must remain in the forefront of our minds. Those who may prove to be beneficial to you this Season must be cultivated however much we despise their origins. Illustrious forebears have not helped your cousin one jot. Send for Amanda, dear. She can read to me until it is time to dress for dinner. Ah, yes, I am persuaded, Lady Glendarvon was most impressed by you today. . . ."

It was growing dark when Lord Glendarvon's yellow high-perch phaeton thundered into the carriage drive of his Park Lane mansion.

He jumped down the moment it stopped and handed the ribbons to the waiting lackey. He strode into the house, immediately handing his whip, gloves and hat to his house-steward and was told, "Her ladyship is in the upstairs drawing-room, my lord, and wishes to see you the moment you arrive home."

"How like her to be so impatient," the marquis remarked, pausing to smooth down his broadcloth coat. "However, an order from her is not to be ignored." As he started up the curved staircase he glanced upwards to see a small white face peering down at him through the bannister rail on the landing. "Veronica, what are you doing hiding there?"

"Waiting for you, of course," the girl replied and then ran down to fling herself at him.

He swung her off her feet, much to her delight, not setting her down until they reached the top. "How heavy you have become," he complained. "Soon I shall be unable to lift you at all."

The girl laughed and clung onto his hand. "Will you come to the schoolroom and read to me for a while?"

"Presently, but for now I am summoned by your mama no doubt for a setdown."

Again Veronica laughed. "Mama would not dare."

"We both know full well that she would. Go along to your room. It is cold on this landing and if you take a chill your mama is bound to chastise me for it. I shall join you presently."

"You do promise?" the girl asked, looking up at him.

"Yes, I promise, but only if you go along *now*."

Satisfied the girl skipped away, watched by the marquis who smiled indulgently. When he went to find Lady Glendarvon she was ensconced by the fire in her own drawing-room furnished in the style of the Sun King. Dainty gilded chairs upholstered in green velvet were ranged around the room to match the scroll-ended sofas near the fire. Limoges china stood on inlaid tables and Lady Glendarvon's slippered feet rested on a tapestry stool.

"My lady," said the marquis as he entered the room which was an excellent backdrop for the elegant Cecilia Glendarvon. "You wished to see me, I understand."

"Always, Fane," she responded, holding out a hand to him.

He walked across the room and, taking her proffered hand, he first raised it to his lips and then placed a kiss upon her cheek. "You look quite ravishing this evening."

"Coming from the much-pursued Fane Glendarvon, that is praise indeed."

"When did any woman compare favourably with you, Cecilia?" he asked, his eyes sparkling with mischief.

"La! You are such a flatterer. Do sit down. I would have a coze with you."

"That sounds decidedly ominous," he replied, seating himself at the other end of the sofa, facing her. "Nothing is amiss with Veronica, I trust."

"Veronica is fine. I met Lady Rishworth this morning when I was in Bond Street. Lorimer's have the most delightful muslins and lustrings just arrived . . ."

"Cecilia . . ." the marquis said in a warning tone.

She smiled. "Georgina Rishworth informed

me, much to my surprise, that Miss Amanda Westwood had returned to London." She glanced at the marquis whose expression had not changed. "You do recall Miss Westwood, do you not?"

"How could I possibly forget? I recall very well that Tomkins was obliged to work for all of two hours polishing my boots before the imprint of her shoe could be removed. When I told Brummel of it he was shocked."

Lady Glendarvon smiled. "When I heard the news of her return I felt it incumbent upon me to seek her out, which I did on the pretext of calling upon Lady Devine."

"I trust you found Miss Westwood in the rudest health," he said, his voice heavy with irony.

"She is no longer a wilful twelve-year-old. Miss Westwood is now some twenty years, and I am bound to say she is uncommonly civil. In truth I half expected a screaming termagant, foaming at the mouth. Nothing could be further from the truth. Not only is she civil, the chit is quite handsome if a trifle dowdy. Her gown was at the very least several seasons old, which was no surprise to me, for I am confident Lady Devine is as close as wax and will not allow the chit any funds at all. I dare say Miss Westwood could afford a basic wardrobe of clothes if she so desired, but she is sorely in need of guidance. Lady Devine is herself a dowd and Miss Rose Devine is nothing more than a goosecap."

"Cecilia, my dear," the marquis said, exhibiting the utmost patience. "I am truly glad to hear that Miss Westwood has garnered a modicum of civility during her exceeding costly sojourn at the academy."

Lady Glendarvon clucked her tongue. "Sarcasm does you no credit, Fane. Are you aware that Miss Westwood was employed as a tutor by Miss Millbeck after her education ended? I can only assume the reason she did so was either because she could not face life at her uncle's house, or more like because the Devines did not want her there."

The marquis laughed. "Do you blame them? Sir Giles confided to me that he was almost killed by a vessel sent flying by that branding-iron. He also confided other misdeeds which I will not trouble to communicate to you at this moment."

"Tush. That was so long ago, my dear. I insist that you postpone judgement until you have met her."

"Oh, Cecilia, pray save me from such a dire fate. If this is what you wished to speak to me about, you can consider me informed, and there's an end to the matter."

He brought out a diamond encrusted snuffbox from which he took a pinch. Lady Glendarvon waited for him to return the box to his pocket before continuing.

"I had not thought you so hard, Fane. Indeed, I know you are not. Miss Westwood's plight has touched my heart. Lady Devine has her as an unpaid lackey. She fetches and carries, and is harangued for her pains."

"How can you possibly judge the situation after so short a visit?"

"Do you think me a chuckle-head, Fane. I have solicited the opinion of others on the matter and they have observed the situation just as I do."

"Well, your concern certainly does you credit, but what can be done? I confess I have no notion what you intend although I am certain you do have something in mind. Would you have me speak to Sir Giles on the matter?"

"It did occur to me that we—you, dear Fane—might see your way to providing a modest portion so she may enjoy a Season and make a respectable match."

"Hell's teeth!" the marquis exclaimed. "Have you windmills in your head, Cecilia? Why should we—I—be so crack-brained?"

Lady Glendarvon put one hand up against his anger. "Fane, do not, I beg of you, harangue me over this. You have, after all, made yourself responsible for Sir Cedric Westwood, and it is merely his sister to whom I refer."

The marquis got to his feet and walked slowly towards the fire, turning his back on it to face the marchioness. "As far as young Cedric is concerned my responsibility will end as soon as he comes down, and none too soon that will be, I am bound to confess. That young man is showing suspicious signs of becoming a scapegrace."

Lady Glendarvon smiled wryly. "Oh, what young man of that age does not?"

"I do trust he will grow out of it in time."

Slyly she added, "At his age you were considered to be a trifle wild yourself."

He smiled at her fondly. "How unkind of you to remind me."

"Your father often despaired of you. Come now, what do you think of this notion of mine?"

The marquis drew himself up to his not inconsiderable height and clasped his hands behind his back. "I consider it a foolish one, if you wish me to be absolutely blunt, my dear."

"Oh, by all means do. You always are, I recall. What a pity you cannot find it in you to agree with me on this matter. The modest portion involved would be a mere bagatelle to you."

"I will not argue with you on that score, but it really would be a cork-brained thing to do. I cannot conceive that you have thought on it properly, my dear."

"The matter has been teasing me since my visit to the Devines. I have thought about nothing else."

"Have you considered the fact that this Season sees the come-out of Miss Westwood's cousin, a vapid miss but one with a substantial portion? How do you imagine the Devines would feel when their poor relative is suddenly an heiress?"

"In all honesty, Fane, I do not care a fig what the Devines would make of it. Miss Westwood is all who concerns me at the moment."

"What would the tattle-baskets make of it, I wonder?"

"It would be easy to think up some Banbury Tale," she responded, sensing a softening of his resolve. "Mayhap we could let it be known that Sir Nigel made provisions for his daughter's portion, untouched by his gaming losses," she went on to suggest.

"It won't do, Cecilia. Everyone knows the Westwood offspring were left penniless by their father's dissolute ways, and I should like to add that Lady Devine herself is mainly responsible for that news being broadcast about the Town."

"There would be pitfalls, I own. . . ."

"Chief among them my distaste for encouraging some poor buck to take a virago for a wife. I could not in all conscience do so."

"You surely cannot still blame Miss Westwood for childish behaviour borne out of misery," Lady Glendarvon chided. "Recall how bewildered and unhappy she must have been. Her entire world had collapsed and she had lost the one person who adored her. I thank God Veronica is not in that situation."

"We cannot compare Veronica's situation with that of Miss Amanda Westwood."

"Well, I know what it is to be poor, Fane. Think on it a moment, how much worse it must be for poor Miss Westwood, who has known wealth and privilege to be obliged to fetch and carry for Lady Devine with not a word of gratitude and no hope of anything better."

"I imagine it is a humbling experience," he admitted with no sign of regret. "And if you wish to make further reference to Sir Cedric, may I tell you that he at least is grateful for all I do on his behalf, which I very much doubt could be said of his sister."

"There is no doubt about Sir Cedric's gratitude. He looks up to you as a God, which must do great wonders for your vanity. Mayhap if Miss Westwood was so adoring. . . ."

Lord Glendarvon looked outraged. "Heaven forbid!" A moment later his expression softened. "Oh, very well, Cecilia. I have the greatest misgivings on this score, but it is evident to me that you are intent upon having your way in this matter and," he added, going to sit by her side and taking her hand, "you know full well I can deny you nothing."

She laughed as he raised her hand to his lips. "I ask only a small amount to be set aside, sufficient to see her respectably wed to some fellow. The Devines could not possibly object to that, I feel."

"From what I have observed of them I would not be so sure. They do not possess your generosity of spirit, but I suspect you already know that." His eyes were full of suppressed laughter as they met hers. "You are truly about to enjoy yourself thoroughly, are you not, Cecilia?"

"I am indeed," she answered with considerably relish. "This Season now promises to be the most lively I can recall in many a long year. Do tell me, Fane, what manner of portion do you think will suffice to see her respectably married?"

"If I am to stump the blunt for this chit, I cannot conceive why it should not be for a substantial sum. After all Miss Westwood has a distinguished line and if you are to take her up, as I am sure you will, we cannot see her married to anyone who is not equally well-bred."

"What do you have in mind?"

"If you tell me who is the greatest heiress on offer this Season, I will stump up something in excess of that portion."

The marchioness both gasped and laughed at the same time. "What a funster you are, Fane. La! 'Tis most amusing, but let us be serious. We are talking of Miss Westwood's future no less."

"Precisely. And, Cecilia, I am not funning."

Once again Lady Glendarvon gasped, her eyes opening wide. "Oh, you cannot possibly mean that."

"Indeed I do."

"I did not intend to elevate her to such a status, Fane. I had in mind for her an impoverished younger son or some such person."

"I will not be accused as being as close as wax. Why should Miss Westwood not be an heiress of means? No doubt the late Sir Nigel Westwood intended that she should. He made it so easy for me to win his property I have since then suffered a sense of shame."

"I would not have believed it of you, my dear. And there are those who maintain that you have no heart. Of course those who do are usually vaporish females who leave your affections untouched."

"So you do not cry off?" he challenged, eyeing her carefully.

"Did you expect that I would?" He laughed and she accused, "You fiend! You did. You hoped I *would* cry off."

"It may well be that even with so great a fortune dangling before them no gentleman of any sensibility would wish to become leg-shackled to such a harpy."

"Where a fortune is concerned there are few enough men of such sensibility, Fane," the marchioness replied wryly. "There will be a stampede I am certain. She really is quite a beauty. You are bound to note it for yourself." Suddenly she looked thoughtful. "Funds will have to be made available to dress her properly. She cannot come-out as shabby as she is at present."

"It is very evident you will not be bored this Season, my dear," the marquis noted wryly. "Let Miss Westwood aspire to the highest in the land. I would not be surprised to see her leg-shackled to a duke. Indeed, we have a clutch of royal princes whose pockets are always to let. Mayhap we shall witness Miss Westwood become Her Royal Highness Princess Amanda. I wonder what the Devines would make of that."

Lady Glendarvon laughed merrily until the tears began to stream down her cheeks.

"Even now I cannot believe I have agreed to this madcap scheme," he told her. "Tomorrow I shall wake up in Bedlam and know I deserve to be there. The truth is, you always bewitch me, Cecilia. Father warned me to beware of your ways."

She laughed again and they were still laughing together when the door opened a crack to reveal Veronica standing there in her night shift. "You promised to read me a story," she said in a reproachful voice.

Immediately the marquis was on his feet. "I

shall come now, my dear. Let no one every say Fane Glendarvon breaks his word." He bent low over the marchioness's hand. "I leave you to your plotting, my dear."

She cast him a grateful look. "I am so very pleased, and I do thank you on Miss Westwood's behalf. No doubt, one day when she is happily settled she will do so herself."

As he hurried across the room towards the child Lord Glendarvon cast the marchioness a wry glance. "Do not be so certain, my dear. Even now I have a fear I may come to regret it."

As the door closed behind them, Lady Glendarvon sank back into the cushions of the sofa her mind frantically at work. Bringing Amanda Westwood out into Society where she belonged was going to be the most diverting experience, she decided.

FIVE

Rose Devine peered out of the window of the first-floor drawing-room of her parents Blooms-bury Square house. "Mama!" she cried. "A carriage is stopping outside the house. I wonder who has come to call."

"Mayhap Captain Collings is calling to leave some geegaw for you, dear."

"Oh no. Captain Collings would come on his horse or in his curricle, I fancy."

"I did have it in mind that Lady Rishworth would call. Oh, by the by, Amanda," Lady Devine glanced across the room to where the girl was intent upon her sewing, "I have asked my maidservant to put some of poor Sophia's gowns in your room. You may find them of use. Naturally, poor Sophia was somewhat thinner than you, but I do not doubt you will be able to make some alterations, for I have observed you a competent with a needle."

A look of horror crossed Amanda's face but she was spared the trouble of replying by her cousin who said, "It is not Lady Rishworth's carriage, Mama. This one is far more elegant, but I cannot see the escutcheon from here. Oh dear, Mama. Lady Glendarvon has alighted from the carriage and she is coming here!"

The needle jabbed into Amanda's finger and she sucked at it, her heart racing for no good reason. Lady Devine immediately began to straighten her cap and look around the room in some agitation.

"There! Did I not tell you her ladyship was taken with you, Rose? Let me look at you."

The girl twirled around, holding out her skirts. "Last time I spoke with Lord Glendarvon he said I was the most vacuous young lady he had ever encountered," she giggled. "He said I could perfect it as an art."

Amanda stared at her in astonishment. "Did that *please* you, Rose?"

All at once her cousin looked haughty. "Indeed, it did. Praise from the Marquis of Glendarvon is not easily won."

"Praise," Amanda murmured in bewilderment, although a quick flare of anger rose inside her at the marquis's arrogance.

"Oh yes, you look fetching," her mother decided. "While Lady Glendarvon is here you must play and sing to her. Your voice is delightful. Everyone is agreed upon that score."

"Mama, Lord Glendarvon has got out of the carriage and is following her inside!"

Immediately Amanda jumped to her feet, her mouth dry, her heart pounding even harder now. "Aunt Ambrosia, may I be excused? I have been endeavouring to write a letter for days, and I believe I can be spared while you receive your visitors."

Lady Devine scarcely glanced at her niece. "Oh yes indeed, Amanda. Do go, for it would not do if Lord Glendarvon claps eyes upon you. It cannot do your cousin's aspirations any good at all for him to be reminded you are a relative. A man such as he will not easily forget your abominable behaviour."

"Be assured I would not kick him again whatever the provocation," Amanda couldn't help but retort as she hurried across the room, her sewing in her hand. "That would be most unseemly, would it not?"

Rose put two hands to her perfectly arranged curls. "Do I truly look fetching, Mama? Only Lord Glendarvon always makes me tremble so with that stare of his, and he is so fastidious in his own appearance and that of his companions."

"Don't fuss, child. Just behave in your normal manner and all will be well. They will both be enchanted with you. I foresee no difficulty obtaining vouchers for Almacks this Season."

All at once Rose's eyes grew bright with speculation. "Mama, do you . . . is it at all possible that Lady Glendarvon has brought his lordship here because . . . ?"

"Hush, Rose dear," her mama chided, her own eyes bright, "all will be clear in good time. You haven't even come out as yet, but I shouldn't be at all surprised at whatever will transpire. Oh, Amanda, before you go plump these cushions and adjust that screen properly. I don't know why we employ servants."

Amanda was obliged to halt her headlong

flight to do her aunt's bidding and just as she reached the door at last it swung open and one of Sir Gile's footmen strode in. "The Marquis and Marchioness of Glendarvon, ma'am."

Amanda stepped back sharply, her eyes downcast, as the couple swept past her into the drawing-room. Her eyes were level with the marchioness's velvet-braided skirt and ironically with Lord Glendarvon's highly-polished hessians, the tassels of which swung hypnotically before her eyes. As they brushed past Amanda pressed herself against the wall in the faint hope she would not be noticed by the visitors.

Lady Devine and her daughter were beaming in anticipation of the visit and they curtseyed deeply. "This is a very great honour," Amanda's aunt murmured as she straightened up. "Lady Glendarvon pray sit by me, and Lord Glendarvon mayhap you would care to sit by Rose. I am persuaded you two would enjoy a coze. You and Rose always deal well together."

The marquis ignored Lady Devine's invitation and remained standing, leaving Rose to sit alone on the sofa, her cheeks unusually pink, her eyes downcast.

Just as Amanda was about to leave the room, believing her presence thankfully overlooked, Lady Glendarvon turned to look at her. "Miss Westwood, I entreat you to remain with us."

"My niece has a good deal to do, my lady," Lady Devine assured her as Amanda looked startled by the request.

"In any event I would be gratified if she would stay and keep us company."

Lady Devine looked most displeased as she said, "Amanda, do come back and sit down."

Still Amanda hesitated by the door but then she came further into the room, still clutching her sewing. The marquis raised his quizzing glass to scrutinise her with the utmost thoroughness for what seemed to be an endless time. She had never felt more vulnerable, aware as never before of her shabby appearance. Still cringing beneath his scrutiny Amanda went to sit by the window, as far from the others as she could contrive, wishing more than ever that she was back at Aylsford.

"Rose has been practising a new song," Lady Devine was saying. "She would be more than delighted to sing it for you. I'm persuaded you would wish to be the first to hear it."

Amanda sighed and applied herself to her sewing as Lord Glendarvon said in the laconic tones she recalled very well, "Do not trouble yourself, Miss Devine. Let it be a pleasure to anticipate."

Rose's cheeks grew even more pink. How foolish she is, Amanda thought. How loathsome was the marquis who made no attempt to hide his contempt for everyone. Her aunt and cousin had no notion of it. Amanda thought her dislike of him had long since abated but seeing him again brought all her resentment to the forefront once more. She recognised that he remained a handsome man without any signs of the hoped-for dissipation about his person. It was most unfair for she didn't doubt he must indulge his desires excessively. As far as appearance went he and the marchioness were well suited and presented a handsome couple.

"You are well settled in London now, Miss Westwood?" the marchioness enquired.

"Yes indeed, I thank you," Amanda replied, averting her eyes for every time she looked up it seemed that the marquis was watching her.

It suddenly occurred to her that the object of his visit was just to see what kind of a creature she had turned out to be, and as the thought crossed her mind her cheeks grew red. If it were so, nothing could be more humiliating.

The marquis continued to prowl around the room, pausing from time to time to examine an ornament or a painting with great interest. As he neared Amanda she became even more nervous, allowing the needle to jab into her finger on several occasions.

"Lady Devine," the marchioness began, glancing at Lord Glendarvon briefly, "I feel we should not mince words. Glendarvon and I came here with a particular purpose in mind. . . ."

Lady Devine began to look as flustered as her niece felt. "My dear Lady Glendarvon, as honoured as we are I feel it incumbent upon me to point out that my dear daughter has not as yet made her debut. . . ."

Lady Glendarvon laughed lightly. "Let me immediately make myself clear. The purpose of our visit here today concerns Miss Westwood, not Miss Devine."

The embroidery fell from Amanda's trembling fingers to the floor but before she could retrieve it the marquis stooped down and picked it up. As he handed it back his eyes met hers for a long moment. How well she recalled the mockery she saw there now, but she could not in all honesty understand it unless their sole reason for this visit was to enable him to gloat over her enforced servitude, but somehow she could not imagine Lady Glendarvon guilty of collusion in something so cruel.

The marquis straightened up and walked away from Amanda who felt she could breathe again.

"Miss Westwood!" her aunt cried, her voice becoming shrill. "I cannot begin to conceive what can concern Miss Westwood. Lord Glendarvon's concern for my niece has long since lapsed."

"You are quite mistaken about that," the marquis replied, turning on his heel to face them again and Amanda fixed her frightened gaze upon him. "My concern for your nephew and niece cannot possibly lapse before they each reach their majority."

"My dear," said the marchioness, addressing Amanda who quickly transferred her startled gaze to Lady Glendarvon, "Glendarvon and I feel it would only be proper for you too to have a Season."

Lady Devine gasped with shock and a little cry emanated from Rose too while Lord Glendarvon surveyed them all down his long, aristocratic nose.

"I cannot possibly," Amanda declared returning her attention to her sewing.

"The chit has not a penny piece," Lady Devine said in disgust while her daughter remained wide-eyed, scarcely able to draw her horrified gaze away from the marquis who appeared to remain totally aloof from the proceedings. "And I can assure you Sir Giles has no more funds available for such a venture. George and Henry are still at Harrow, so you must see that a come-out for Miss Westwood is totally out of the question."

When the marquis began to address them again, as on that long-ago day in the lawyer's chambers he commanded the attention of all those present the moment he started to speak. "The question of money is of no real consequence, Lady Devine. A portion will be provided. When Sir Nigel was foolish enough to leave his children penniless, it seemed that I would be obliged to look out for them. And so I shall. Sir Cedric has an allowance and will be given title to the house in Mount Street as and when he displays sufficient sense to manage his own affairs."

Although Amanda resented bitterly his arrogance she could not in all honesty question the good sense of what he said of Cedric.

"It is no secret, I believe, that in my hands Sir Nigel's fortune has grown considerably," the marquis was saying, "and in all conscience I feel I should bestow some of it upon his daughter. . . ."

Angered now beyond reason by his pompous utterings Amanda jumped to her feet. "Enough of this!" she cried. "Do what you will for my

85

brother, but pray leave me alone. I want nothing from you."

"For once I am obliged to agree with my niece, my lord," her aunt said, clutching one hand to her chest in a gesture that looked decidedly ominous to Amanda. "You must see that she is neither prepared nor suited to a Season."

"I cannot agree with you upon that," Lady Glendarvon gently interpolated, her manner utterly at odds with that of the marquis. "Miss Westwood's plain-spoken way could be interpreted by some as refreshing, I fancy."

What was suddenly very evident to Amanda was the fact that Lady Glendarvon was enjoying the situation hugely, but exactly whose discomfiture she was relishing there was no way of knowing.

"Come now, you cannot truly enjoy your present situation, Miss Westwood," the marquis chided, to Amanda's further annoyance.

"I cannot conceive why you think I do not," she replied, her eyes ablaze, her head held high.

Drawing a sigh he sat down at last and Lady Glendarvon turned to Lady Devine who appeared mortified by the very idea her niece be given a Season. "Lady Devine why not think on how this may affect your own daughter."

"Rose? I cannot begin to think what this has to do with my daughter, ma'am, truly I cannot."

"Miss Rose will no doubt require vouchers to attend Almacks, will she not?" Both Lady Devine and her daughter looked wide-eyed and a little fearful at the marchioness who went on after a telling pause. "I am well acquainted with both Lady Jersey and Countess Lieven. Favour in their eyes is necessary to gain entry which is most important to any girl just come-out into Society, but I do not suppose Miss Devine is like to have any difficulty obtaining vouchers to that most exclusive of places."

There was, for a moment or two after she had finished speaking, a most resounding silence and then the marquis got to his feet and addressed Lady Glendarvon. "My dear, we have put the matter to Lady Devine. Mayhap we should now depart and allow her and Miss Westwood to think on the matter."

As the marchioness got to her feet Amanda said passionately, "I shall not be put up as a Smithfield Bargain, my lady."

"It is inconceivable that any gentleman would wish to marry you for the benefit of the portion alone," Lady Glendarvon pointed out. "A Season is only your due. Do not allow your prejudice to blind you to it."

Amanda was scarcely aware of their leave-taking but after they had gone Lady Devine sank back onto her sofa emitting a cry. Amanda knew she should go to minister to her aunt but she just couldn't move, nor could she think or feel to any great degree. She could only recall the cold, impersonal look in the marquis's eyes. As proud as Lucifer, she thought, but what had prompted him to make such an offer? No doubt Lady Glendarvon had something to do with the matter, but the notion they might look upon her in a charitable light was quite mortifying.

Rose rushed across to her shocked mother, crying, "Mama, what does it mean?"

Lady Devine put one hand to her head. "I declare I am all a mort, but it appears if you are to be launched into the *ton* this Season you will be obliged to share your come-out with Amanda. If we do not agree I am persuaded Lady Glendarvon would bar your way to Almacks."

Rose let out a high-pitched shriek, stamping her foot on the floor. Then she wheeled round on her cousin. "You sly creature. How can you do this to me?"

"I had no notion of this!" Amanda protested, but her cousin was too far gone in her anger to listen.

Once again Rose stamped her foot on the floor. "Don't seek to gammon me. You have been greasing Lady Glendarvon's boots. I have witnessed your toady-ing ways with my own eyes. Why did I not see you for the shabby creature you are? How cork-brained of me to believe you had changed your ways. You are as wicked as we always thought."

"Rose," Amanda pleaded. "How can you say this when I am as shocked as you? This is only the second time I have seen Lady Glendarvon and never in private. I cannot possibly have been greasing her boots and you know it as well as I."

"What nonsense! I see it now. You have set your cap at Lord Glendarvon. As if he would consider such a dowd as you when the most dazzling beauties in the land have not been able to bring him up to scratch."

Amanda was so shocked by this accusation she laughed out loud. "This has all the makings of a Drury Lane comedy. Rose, have you taken leave of your senses? I declare that someone has. How can anyone set their cap at Lord Glendarvon when he is already wed?"

At last Lady Devine sat up, rallying slightly. "Wed? To whom is he wed pray tell me?"

"Lady Glendarvon, naturally. I declare we are all fit for Bedlam."

Lady Devine began to laugh in a high-pitched manner which exuded no merriment. "I own the tattle-baskets have a great deal to say on that score, especially with regard to little Lady Veronica, but Lady Glendarvon is the marquis's stepmother. I thought you of all people would know that."

Amanda's head reeled with the knowledge her aunt had imparted. His stepmother! The dowager Lady Glendarvon. It was she who had chosen Miss Millbeck's Academy. The harridan of her imagination was the delightful Cecilia Glendarvon.

As Amanda sank back down on the chair in order to digest this information, Lady Devine let out a little cry and fell back onto the cushions. "La! This has all been too much for me. I scarce know what to think. I am quite overset."

Rose cast a venomous look in Amanda's direction. "Can you not see that Mama is having an attack of the vapours? Fetch her vinaigrette with no further delay. We may even have to burn feathers!" When Amanda made no effort to move Rose urged, "Hurry do, you lazy creature."

The tone of her cousin's voice snapped Amanda out of her reverie and she retorted, "Fetch it yourself, Rose. After all that has happened today I have much thinking to do."

"The ingratitude," Lady Devine gasped. "I have nurtured a viper in my bosom, but I should not be surprised for I always suspected it was so. Rose, fetch a quill and paper. I must pen a note to Lady Glendarvon to warn her of the treacherousness of this creature. In no circumstances can I allow your come-out year to be ruined by that hoyden."

When Amanda reached the door she glanced back at her aunt and cousin who seemed truly distressed, and cast them a sincere look of regret before letting herself out of the room.

SIX

The rain had ceased but the street still gleamed and the trees in the square dripped steadily. Amanda stood at the window of her bedchamber, staring out at the miserable scene which mirrored the feeling in her heart. Although several days had passed since the marquis and his stepmother had called the atmosphere had not lightened one bit. The entire family behaved as if it was Amanda's own personal plan to upstage Rose. Even Sir Giles had begun to treat her with an uncharacteristic coolness.

Moreover, since Lady Devine had been indisposed, responsibility for all their social activities had fallen upon Amanda who, for once, was far too preoccupied to give her full attention to all that was involved. Characteristically her aunt had embarked upon a programme of diversions to make Rose's come-out spectacular, but without any real thought as to the work involved. Amanda thought that someone like Lady Glendarvon could probably cope with any number of social activities in her home, but Aunt Ambrosia was made of less stern stuff.

Since the visit of Lord and Lady Glendarvon it seemed to Amanda that her situation here was more intolerable than before. She was in an invidious situation, torn between her family, which in any event treated her with barely disguised hostility, and the enigma of Lord Glendarvon who seemed set upon fulfilling what he believed to be his duty. Each circumstance was equally intolerable to her. Never before had Amanda longed more for the simplicity of life at Aylsford, and now she faced the very real possibility that it was lost to her for ever.

When a carriage drew up outside the house, disgorging a man she recognised as her aunt's physician, Amanda walked away from the window to a table where several notes to Lady Glendarvon remained half-written and abandoned. The marchioness and her stepson had refused to listen to her verbal protestations, no doubt not believing the veracity of them, so it seemed unlikely they would heed a polite refusal which came by way of a note.

Feeling totally exasperated Amanda scooped up the crumpled notes and threw them into the grate, watching them flare up and turn black. When she heard Dr. Knox's carriage depart she ran down the stairs to encounter the house-steward bearing a recently delivered letter addressed to her. Amanda had, naturally, replied to Lucy's last letter and in all honesty had not looked for a reply so soon. Curious, she tore at the wafer and to her further surprise what proved to be a banker's draft fell out. It was for fifty guineas drawn on Coutt's Bank. The money had never been more welcome, but she eagerly scanned the page in search of its origins. As she read Lucy's familiar hand Amanda couldn't help but gasp.

My dearest Amanda she began, I am persuaded you will be most surprised if not utterly shocked at what has transpired. Immediately after your departure for London I took the liberty of forwarding The Terrors of Lucifer *to Mr. Long of the Minerva Press and he has now declared his wish to publish it. I hope you will not be angry with me, dearest, for I could not be more delighted for you. Needless to add he intends to respect your wish for anonymity. . . .*

Amanda's head reeled, for she was beginning to think she must be in the grip of a virulent nightmare. *The Terrors of Lucifer* to be published? She could scarce believe it possible that anyone would consider her childish ramblings suitable for public reading. Even though she intended to try and stop publication she was heartily grateful for the whim that made her attach another name to the tome.

When her cousin came into the hall Amanda swiftly folded both the letter and the draft, hiding it in her hand. "Rose, how is Aunt Ambrosia today?"

Amanda's polite enquiry was met with a glacial stare. "Dr. Knox declares Mama's nerves are entirely overset, and we all know to whom we must attribute the blame."

"Rose, that is a nonsense. I am as disturbed as anyone about this matter. I had no notion

Lady Glendarvon was about to make such a ludicrous proposal. You must be aware that I want nothing from the Glendarvons."

Rose did not trouble to reply. She turned on her heel and apparently went to minister to her distraught mother. Watching her go, Amanda drew a sigh of resignation and hastily hurried to her room, which was rapidly becoming her only haven. For a long while she paced the floor, seeing no way out of the dilemma except perhaps for one.

Very softly she put her few belongings into a cloakbag, regretfully leaving all her precious books where they were. If all went well she would be able to send for them later. Amanda tied on her old blue velvet bonnet and her one warm palisse before picking up the cloakbag. She was able to make her way down the back stairs and out of the servants' entrance without being seen. With Lady Devine on her sickbed it was certain those servants not involved in making and serving dinner would be dancing attendance on the invalid.

As she hurried through the square Amanda was thankful not to be encountered by any of the Devines' many acquaintances or neighbours. Then, once clear of Bloomsbury Square, she sought a hackney carriage, but all those which swept past appeared to be engaged and Amanda was resolved to walk the entire distance to *The Old Swan*.

To add to her misery as she reached Oxford Street the rain began to come down once again. At first it was just a few drops but quickly it became a steady drizzle and within a very few minutes quite a downpour. The fashionables climbed into their carriages and sped home, leaving the pavements deserted although the street was full of clattering wheels and pounding hooves. Even the inveterate peddlers had somehow found shelter and no longer filled the streets with their raucous cries.

Reaching Bond Street with the rain fast seeping through the material of her gown Amanda started across the road, only to jump back as a curricle went by at a fast pace. When she started across again the rain blinding her, another carriage thundered past, splashing her already soaked gown with filthy water. The shock of the drenching caused her to lose her grip on the cloakbag which flew into the road to be run over by another passing carriage. Amanda cried out in vexation and dashed forward to retrieve her sodden belongings before any worse ill befell them. As she did so she only narrowly missed slipping beneath the wheels of a phaeton, sitting down in the gutter instead.

Realising what a sorry spectacle she must present she was oblivious to the fact that the wet was soaking through her clothes to her skin. Tears began to roll down her cheeks to mingle with the raindrops which continued to beat down on her bedraggled figure. Amanda wasn't even aware that the phaeton had stopped and its driver was walking back towards her.

"What do you think you are about?" an angry voice demanded. "How foolish can anyone be? You were almost killed by your madcap behaviour. Do you hear me, madam?" Amanda raised her rain and tear-stained face to find herself looking at the angry features of Lord Glendarvon. "Miss Westwood!" he cried, genuinely shocked by the state he had found her in. "Do allow me to assist you."

Bending down he tried to raise her from the gutter only to be told, "Leave me alone, I pray of you, my lord." Her voice was imploring but not raised above a whisper.

"To do so would be an act of criminal folly," he retorted and suddenly Amanda had the insane desire to giggle at the sight of the rain dripping off his high-crowned beaver as he bent over her.

Despite her declared reluctance to be assisted he lifted her easily to her feet and before she could utter any further protest he was propelling her through the puddles and handing her onto the box of his phaeton where she could not help but feel glad of the shelter available. He had also retrieved her sodden cloakbag which he flung behind the box, exhibiting great distaste. The moment he climbed up beside her he took the ribbons and whipped the team into action.

"Why are you abroad on such a foul day?" he asked after a moment, glancing at her briefly.

"I was going about some errands for my aunt," she replied in a muted tone.

He laughed much to her mortifications as he skilfully handled his magnificent team of horses. "I do not believe even Lady Devine could be so hard-hearted as to send you abroad on foot on a day like this."

"It is evident you do not hold my family in high regard, my lord."

"In all honesty, Miss Westwood, I consider they have used you ill."

"It is understandable. I have not always appreciated their charity and no one likes a poor relation."

He clucked his tongue. "Where is the spirited Miss Westwood I recall so clearly?"

"She has become a realist, my lord."

"You disappoint me. However, we have still not ascertained where you were bound." When she remained silent, he went on, "Allow me to hazard a guess if you are not to be forthcoming. You were clutching a cloakbag . . ."

"Some clothes to distribute to the poor," she interpolated.

Again he laughed, much to her chagrin. "Miss Westwood, would even the poor want your cast-off clothing?"

Furious now, Amanda turned on him. "How ungallant you are, Lord Glendarvon. I confess my apparel is not all the crack, but I make no apology for that. . . ."

"You would disappoint me if you did, Miss Westwood. From what I observed you must have been making for Piccadilly where there are several coaching inns." Once again he paused to glance at her and she remained silent, fearing that she would never contrive to beat him in any way. "The Gloucester stage leaves from *The Old Swan*. You could hire a wagon to take you from Gloucester to Aylsford, could you not?"

Amanda considered it prudent to set aside her pride, for it did not weigh with him. All those years ago she had correctly designated him a devil and it was now clear to her he had not changed.

"My lord, if you wish to do me a kindness and save yourself trouble and expense I beg of you take me there right now."

"In those clothes, my dear Miss Westwood, you would soon contract some fearful ague which might even endanger your life."

Amanda's head drooped. "I do not care," she said in a voice no more than a whisper.

"I regret I cannot in all conscience aid you in such a foolhardy scheme."

"Be damned to your conscience!" she cried, rallying once more and he looked at her in alarm. Amanda quickly averted her face. "Where are you taking me?"

"Back to Bloomsbury Square. You cannot travel any further in that sorry state. You must take off your clothes. . . ."

Once again Amanda turned to him. "Do not I beg of you return me there. If you have any feelings at all . . . I cannot bear . . ."

Her voice trailed away as she noted the quick flash of anger which flared in his eyes and that puzzled her somewhat, but her relief was considerable when he replied, "Very well. It shall be as you wish."

He urged on his team, driving down a side street and then into Piccadilly. However when they passed *The Old Swan* Amanda was alarmed now, but before she could question him further the phaeton had turned into Park Lane. The marquis skilfully drove the phaeton into a wide carriage drive in front of one of the mansions which faced Hyde Park. The moment it stopped a lackey stepped forward to take the ribbons. Lord Glendarvon climbed down and then waited for Amanda.

"Come along, Miss Westwood. You will catch your death if you persist on sitting there."

Reluctantly she got up, but as she did so her head began to swim. He held out his hand to her and with even more reluctance she took it, hating even so slight a contact with him. As she swayed once more he disengaged his hand and put both hands around her waist, lifting her down to the ground. At any other time Amanda would have been mortified but just then she felt so odd it did not seem to matter. When he set her down she swayed uncertainly again and he drew her under the portico and into the vast hall of Glendarvon House.

As he stripped off his wet greatcoat and sodden beaver hat he barked orders at the servants who seemed to be scurrying all over the place.

"Wilkins, is her ladyship at home?"

"I regret not, my lord, although we are expecting her back at any time now."

"That's too bad, but we shall have to contrive for the moment without her. See that a fire is lit in one of the bedchambers and instruct a maidservant to fetch hot water and clean clothing for Miss Westwood. Oh yes, Wilkins, see that someone brings up a large jug of porter."

"Yes, my lord."

The house-steward and several footmen hurried off to do the marquis's bidding but not before they cast Amanda disgusted looks. When the marquis looked at her again she was motionless with water dripping from her clothes onto the tessellated marble floor. Feeling somewhat bewildered she glanced around her, at the staircase which swept in two flights to a landing where she thought she noted a pale face peering down at them.

"Come along, Miss Westwood. Why do you delay? Take off your bonnet and pelisse."

When Amanda made no move to obey his instructions he began to untie the ribbons of her bonnet himself and for some reason she could not understand she made no move to stop him even when he unfastened her pelisse and allowed it to fall to the floor. Amanda felt strangely distant from what was happening to her. It was as if she was watching it happening to someone else from a great distance.

"Follow me, Miss Westwood," he ordered in a tone which normally would have angered her with its imperious tone.

Her response to his order was to sneeze and, casting her a wry look the marquis took her by the wrist and led her up the stairs. A child was standing on the landing and she stared at Amanda. The marquis spoke to the child as they went by but Amanda had no notion what he said. She allowed herself to be taken into a bedchamber where a fire was roaring up the chimney. A maidservant was bending over the coals and when Amanda and the marquis entered the girl stepped back dropping into a deep curtsey.

Several other servants arrived, bringing with them hot water, dry clothes and soft towels. The marquis led Amanda towards the fire where, despite the very welcome warmth, she began to sneeze.

"Miss Westwood," he said in a patient tone as he retreated towards the door, "you are soaked to the skin so I will leave you to get out of those wet clothes and into dry ones with no further delay." Amanda stared at him wide-eyed, swaying slightly as he added, coming back towards her, "If you do not take them off right now I shall be obliged to do it for you."

She stepped back from what she perceived to be a very real threat, but all at once he blurred before her.

"I am the most tiresome creature, am I not?" she asked as her knees gave way completely.

"Tiresome indeed," replied the marquis as he caught her in his arms before she reached the floor.

Amanda's last recollection before darkness enfolded her was of being held close to him, and then she knew nothing more.

SEVEN

The room was immediately unfamiliar although delightfully warm. Amanda awoke to find herself in a bed which felt strange and looking up at a tester above her head which she did not recognise. A moment later at the sound of rain pattering persistently at a nearby window she recalled what had happened to her, particularly the humiliation of collapsing into the arms of the Marquis of Glendarvon. When she lifted the covers a little she found herself clad in the finest of lawn bedshifts with no sign of her own clothes to be seen.

As she struggled to sit up in the strange bed a voice said, "So you are awake at last." It was Lady Glendarvon herself who came to the foot of the bed. "Do you feel recovered now, my dear?"

"Yes, I thank you," Amanda replied, fingering the fine Brussels lace at the neck of the bedshift. "How did I come to be here?"

"Do you not recall? Glendarvon found you

in some distress in Bond Street and brought you here."

"Yes, yes, I recall that very well," she answered, not wishing to remember it at all. "It's just that I do not recall getting into bed. I'm persuaded I did not undress myself."

"No, indeed. You have my own maidservant, Nel, to thank for that."

Amanda sank back into the pillows, drawing a sigh of relief. "How long have I been here? It seems to have been a very long time."

"Only since yesterday evening."

"Have I been very ill?"

"Dr. Fenton, whom we called immediately to attend you, says not. You have suffered a severe chill which is not so surprising, but you appear to have a strong constitution. I'm persuaded you are much better now. Your fever has completely gone which is a great relief."

Amanda began to get out of the bed. "I do thank you for your concern, my lady, but I shall not impose upon you a moment longer. Have my clothes been dried?"

Lady Glendarvon came round the bed to ease her back into it, which was, perversely, a great relief to Amanda as she discovered she still felt a little weak. "Your clothes are utterly ruined, but no matter. What is important is you do need further rest. Tell me where you wish to go in such a hurry." Before Amanda could think of something the marchioness went on. "Glendarvon tells me you were bound for Aylsford. Is that so?"

Heavily Amanda sighed, "Yes."

"Does that mean Miss Millbeck keeps the

post open for you whenever you wish to return?"

Looking abashed Amanda could not lie. "No. Aunt Ambrosia contrived that she did not, but Miss Millbeck always held me in the highest esteem, and I hoped she would find some manner of occupation for me." As she spoke her eyes suddenly focused on some familiar boxes in the far corner of the room. "Those are mine," she said in astonishment. "I recall I left them at my uncle's house. How do they come to be *here*?"

Lady Glendarvon sat down by the bed. "My servants brought your possessions from Devine House this morning. I do hope that doesn't anger you."

Shaking her head in bewilderment Amanda replied. "Naturally not, my lady, but why did you do so?"

"When I returned home yesterday and discovered you here I deemed it only correct to pen a note to your relatives to let them know where you were in the event you were missed and they were worried about you. The manner of Lady Devine's reply led me to believe it would be better by far if you remained here at Glendarvon house."

Amanda's eyes grew wide. "Oh, my lady, I cannot possibly do so."

"Why not?"

In all truth, Amanda could not think of an answer to that question but while she sought for one the marchioness went on. "What is almost certain is that you cannot return to Bloomsbury Square with any degree of equanimity. You may read Lady Devine's reply if you have any doubts about that."

"Oh, I can well imagine the contents," Amanda answered wryly, "but it still remains that I cannot impose upon you. . . ."

"It will be a pleasure, I assure you, my dear. We have already achieved, I believe, a fine degree of accord between us."

"It is Lord Glendarvon who concerns me. He cannot possibly agree to having me here in his house."

"I cannot conceive why you should think he would not. Naturally, I would not have embarked upon such a course of action without his agreement. We both consider the Devines unsuited to have you in their care."

"I came to London at Lady Devine's behest with no expectations whatsoever."

Lady Glendarvon smiled at last. "Indeed, I am fully aware of that, and it can only endear you to me." The door opened and a maidservant entered, carrying a tray. "Nel has brought you some of her excellent beef tea, Miss Westwood. Drink it all I entreat you, for it will help to restore your spirits. We have much to do if you are to be launched into Society as is your due with no further delay."

Once again Amanda looked alarmed. "No. Oh no, it is not at all necessary. I beg you to abandon all notions of bringing me out."

"My dear, you have proved admirably your ability to be an independent female. I, too, have been in that situation and I know it is far better to be wealthy and loved. Do not, I beg of you, allow foolish pride to set you on a course for a lonely future. We shall speak again when you feel stronger."

As Amanda watched her walk across the large expanse of floor towards the door she found it difficult to believe Lady Glendarvon had not been wellborn. She had more dignity and breeding than many who were born to the *ton*.

When she had gone Nel set the tray of beef tea before Amanda who began to drink. Musing on what the marchioness had said, she couldn't help but wonder if it was the marquis to whom she referred when she spoke of being loved. Recalling Rose's sly taunts it was very likely and Amanda could not blame him his devotion.

She drank every drop of the beef tea with Nel's gimlet gaze daring her not to. When she had gone and Amanda was left alone again she gladly sank back into the pillows while somewhere inside her, amidst the confusion, was a stirring of excitement.

Amanda was standing by the fire, still wearing Lady Glendarvon's bedshift and over it a matching negligee, when the door opened. She had been musing on the necessity of calling upon Mr. Long of the Minerva Press as soon as was possible. Too many days had passed since receiving the news from Lucy and the banker's draft. If publication was to be stopped she must act with the utmost urgency now.

When she turned towards the door it was to see Lady Glendarvon who was followed closely by her maid who Amanda had discovered was devoted to her mistress.

"You look so much better this morning!" the marchioness declared as she came across the room. "There is colour in your cheeks again. That pallor certainly did not become you."

"Any improvement to my health is due entirely to your excellent nursing, my lady, and Nel's beef tea," she added hastily.

Nel, Amanda noticed belatedly, had been carrying a number of garments when she entered the room and now she placed them carefully on the bed.

"You will wish to dress now you are feeling better," Lady Glendarvon pointed out, "and I have brought you a selection of gowns which I believe will suit until other arrangements can be made."

Amanda could see a velvet day dress, several made out of muslin and sarsenet, and even a satin evening own. "These are far too good," she gasped. "Indeed they look new."

"They are new," the marchioness confirmed. "And why should you not enjoy modish apparel? You are now an heiress of considerable wealth."

The mention of it caused Amanda's cheeks to grow pink. "My lady, once again I must protest. In all truth I have no wish to return to Alysford now there is no place for me there. I harbour even more reluctance to return to my uncle's house, but mayhap you will allow me to remain, if you wish it, to serve you. It would be both an honour and a pleasure, I assure you."

107

Nel clucked her tongue and frowned while the marchioness laughed. "Tush. I am not in the least bit vaporish and therefore need no one to fetch my vinaigrette for me. You will take your rightful place in Society. I am determined upon that, and as for the gowns, I invariably order too many every Season. Nel will alter them to fit until we are able to have some made especially for you."

"I cannot thank you enough for your kindnesses to me." Amanda said in heartfelt tones.

"Stuff and nonsense, my dear. I thank you. I shall enjoy myself hugely, and if thanks are needed you may do so by making a brilliant match. That will be sufficient, I assure you. I was most unhappy when Glendarvon won so much from your father, but he was such a rakehell in those days one could not reason with him, and in truth by the time I came to hear of it the deed was done." She glanced around the room. "I note you have begun to unpack your boxes. There are so many books. I cannot credit it. La! It appears to me I have intervened only just in time before you became a bluestocking!"

Amanda laughed and as she did so she realised it was a very long time since she had felt so light-hearted. If only she could feel some vestige of warmth towards Lord Glendarvon life would be better than it had for years, but all she could recall was his irritation with her and her own hatred which spanned almost half her life. She did not doubt he had agreed to this arrangement because he always deferred to his stepmother's wishes. That knowledge coupled with her own dislike of him would render being in his company a very discomforting experience.

"Oh yes, I almost forgot." The marchioness glanced at her maid. "Hand Miss Westwood the box, Nel." As the woman did so Lady Glendarvon explained, "I considered it prudent to have this brought over from your uncle's house. I trust you will agree with me about that."

She left in a cloud of her own special eau-de-cologne and while Nel sorted the clothes Amanda sat down to open the box, gasping as she set eyes on her mother's jewels for the first time since she was a small child. It was a miracle, she thought, that her father had not lost them at the gaming-tables even before they had passed to Lord Glendarvon. The sight of the pearls, diamonds, sapphires and rubies arranged into pieces of exquisite jewellery, brought tears to her eyes. However reluctant she had been to take up Lady Glendarvon's offer of a Season she had much cause to be grateful for the jewellery being restored to her.

As Lady Glendarvon had promised, the days to follow were indeed hectic, but as soon as Amanda was able to slip away she hired a hackney carriage to take her to the offices of the Minerva Press where she introduced herself to Mr. Long as Lucy Brandfoot.

"I am here as emissary from Miss Emily Godrington," she explained, feeling nervous. "She wishes to return to you the money paid

109

for *The Terrors of Lucifer*, and asks me to have the novel withdrawn."

"My dear Mrs. Brandfoot, would that I could acquiesce to Miss Godrington's wishes," the publisher explained, "but 'tis impossible. The machinery has now been set in motion."

"It *must* be possible to withdraw it. Miss Godrington was emphatic in her instructions to me."

"There is no stopping it now," he assured her and Amanda was aghast. "But you may inform Miss Godrington that *The Terrors of Lucifer* is going to be the greatest success. Mayhap you will be able to persuade her to make herself known," he ventured.

"Oh no," Amanda cried in panic. "That would be impossible." When he gave her a curious look she went on, "Miss Godrington is a timid creature and would not for anything wish for public acclaim."

His face suddenly brightened. "It is unfortunate but we shall be able to build upon that, have no fear. The ladies of the *beau monde* will love the mystery surrounding her and, no doubt, make much of it."

Needless to say, Amanda was not reassured. She made her way back to Glendarvon House feeling stunned, but by the time she arrived she was resigned at last to the inevitability of seeing the novel in print.

Much to her relief her absence had not been missed and she immediately returned to her room to set about arranging it to her satisfaction now that it was certain she would stay. It was not a difficult task, for her bedchamber at

Glendarvon House was much larger than the one allocated her at her uncle's abode. This one had the advantage of a dressing-room, and it overlooked the garden so that she was not disturbed by street noises which could be considerable in Park Lane.

However, even given the size of the room, finding suitable places for all her books was quite a task. Some were piled upon the tables, others she had left packed away in her boxes. Amanda had just picked up one of her old favourites and began to leaf through it when the door opened a fraction.

She straightened up and called, "Do come in," and when the door opened fully an auburn-haired little girl came in. "Hello," Amanda greeted her with a friendly smile.

"You must be Miss Westwood."

"And you are . . ."

The girl came further into the room, curtseying, "Lady Veronica Astleigh."

"As I thought, for you look so much like your mama. You will be a great beauty like her before long."

"Mama tells me you are come to stay, to have a Season, but I cannot conceive why. Are you a relative of ours?"

"No," Amanda answered thoughtfully. "Our families are acquainted though. My mama and papa are dead, so Lady Glendarvon has taken it upon herself to bring me out. It is very good of her."

"My papa is also dead, but my brother is as good as a father on account of his being so

111

much older than I am. Mama is not his mother, of course."

Amanda laughed. "Yes, I know that. You are most fortunate. My brother is younger than I am."

"Sir Cedric Westwood. Of course I do know him and I like him very much. He makes me laugh. One day he took me riding in his curricle and we raced through Hyde Park. It was the greatest fun."

"I had no notion you were so well acquainted with my brother."

"We are more than acquainted, Miss Westwood. I have made Sir Cedric promise to wait until I am old enough to marry him."

Amanda fought hard to contain her amusement. "How old are you?"

"Ten, well almost."

"Sir Cedric has a long wait ahead of him, Lady Veronica. Do you deem it fair to make him promise?"

"He says I am well worth the wait. Even though he sometimes confesses to find me tiresome he says my portion makes it worth the wait."

Amanda did laugh then and the girl skipped about the room interesting herself in all Amanda's belongings. She reminded Amanda of herself at that age, confident and bold, unaware that within a short time her entire world would collapse in ruins.

"You seem inordinately fond of Lord Bryon's work," Lady Veronica remarked at last.

"Yes, indeed I am. Do you read his poems too?"

"As soon as they are published."

"You may borrow any book you like."

"I thank you, but he presented me with my own copy of *Childe Harold's Pilgrimage*."

Amanda was amazed to hear her say so. "Do you actually know Lord Byron?"

"Yes, indeed. You will too, for he is a regular at Mama's soirées. Glendarvon does not care for him overmuch. He says he is effete and my brother cannot forgive him for not being able to tie his neckcloth with any degree of skill. And of course Lord Byron is not a Corinthian so Glendarvon's dislike is quite understandable."

"Your brother, I am persuaded, is a hard man to please," Amanda told her as she applied herself once more to the books.

"That is undoubtedly so." Lady Veronica smiled wickedly. "*Entre nous*, Miss Westwood, I must tell you in general he finds females a trifle tiresome, except for Mama and myself, naturally."

Clutching a book of poetry to her breast, Amanda felt herself stiffening involuntarily. "Lord Glendarvon is too top-lofty for his own good," she murmured.

"No one would dare gainsay you on that score, Miss Westwood. Mama says he is as proud as Lucifer."

"Veronica!" Her mother's voice from the doorway made the child jump. "I do trust you are not tiring Miss Westwood with your chatter."

"Please do not scold her, my lady," Amanda pleased. "I am enjoying her company."

113

"That pleasure must await another day, for we are to go to Bond Street to buy what we need."

"May I go with you, Mama?" the girl entreated. "Do say that I can."

"Only if you promise not to plague us with your endless chattering I might be prevailed upon to allow you to come along."

Lady Veronica jumped up and down with excitement. "I will be as mute as a fish, I vow."

Her mother laughed. "Go then and put on your outdoor clothes and be quick about it."

"Hurrah!" Lady Veronica cried as she rushed out of the room.

"Your daughter is quite delightful, Lady Glendarvon," Amanda told her the moment the child had gone.

The marchioness smiled. "I own that she is. Unfortunately Glendarvon believes that indulging her every whim is the best way to make up for her lack of a parent. I am not so sure although I confess I am rather guilty too."

She came further into the room accompanied by the ever-faithful Nel. "Before we are able to go anywhere we must do something about your hair. The style is most outmoded and needs must be changed with no further delay. Your new outdoor gown and bonnet have arrived from the mantua-maker so you will be able to wear them today."

Amanda put one hand to her hair. "We are only going to Bond Street and the Strand, my lady," she pointed out.

114

"Whenever you appear in public you must strive for perfection. I am determined that you will cause no small commotion in this Town. To work Nel!"

EIGHT

The mercers and haberdashers of Bond Street
and the Strand welcomed Lady Glendarvon
most graciously. It was evident she was a valued customer of all the most fashionable estab-
lishments. The marchioness had a mental list
of all a young lady required for a successful
social Season and what she did forget the vi-
vacious Lady Veronica reminded her. Soon
Amanda's head swam with the sheer variety
of materials set out for her selection. Despite
the war against Napoleon there seemed to
be no shortage of materials brought in from
the East and after much consideration what
seemed to be a prodigious amount of poplin,
chintz, sprigged muslin, velvet and satin were
set aside. After choosing materials they went
on to purchase lace, ribbons, feathers, plumes,
silk stockings, gloves and shawls.

At every establishment they visited eager
eyes were turned in their direction and often
they were obliged to pause in their shopping
while Lady Glendarvon presented Amanda to
Lady Colton, the Duchess of Burford, Countess

Rostoff and many other ladies of the *beau monde*. Amanda took a careful mental note of each of them for future reference but she was very much afraid she would not remember all those she had met. However, everyone encountered displayed a lively interest in her. Amanda could only think that Lady Devine would be furious if she knew.

At one linen draper's warehouse Amanda was amazed to come face to face with a contemporary of hers from the academy. Louisa Kirk had left to embark upon a Season a few years ago and now eagerly informed Amanda that she was married to an officer of hussars, currently in the Peninsula with the Duke of Wellington.

"La! How good it is to see you again," Louisa declared. "I had heard mention that an Amanda Westwood was about to come out with an enormous portion but I could not credit it was you. You must tell me how it has come about. There are so many *on-dits* I scarce know what to believe."

"The matter is very simple, Louisa," Amanda replied, feeling distinctly uncomfortable as she invariably did whenever the portion was mentioned, "Papa charged Lord Glendarvon to bring me out many years ago." It was the story agreed upon with Lady Glendarvon, "Lord Glendarvon was not obliged to do so, of course, but he insisted it should be so."

"Lord Glendarvon must be a prodigious good man," Louisa responded, to Amanda's further discomfiture. "I must leave you now, dearest,

117

but be certain to call upon me at Bedford Square as soon as you are able and we shall have a lengthy coze."

"There, I have told her of why I am being brought out by you, my lady," Amanda told the marchioness when Louisa had departed.

"Good. The story will be all over town within the sen'night and coming as it does from your own lips it will be regarded as the true one."

"Mrs. Bell considers Lord Glendarvon to be something of a hero in the matter," Amanda said, a little resentfully.

The marchioness cast her a wry look. "Whereas you consider him to be rather more of a villan."

Amanda looked shocked. "Oh no, Lady Glendarvon, I would not have you think so."

"That is quite all right, my dear," the marchioness assured her, patting at her hand. "Your feelings are quite understandable. Mayhap they are like to change in the time to come."

Amanda did not reply but she looked doubtful and Lady Veronica, overhearing the conversation added, "How anyone can take Fane in dislike I cannot conceive. Why, half the ladies of the *ton* are in love with him."

"Then it will do him much good to encounter one who isn't," her mother remarked as they climbed back into the carriage.

Lady Glendarvon instructed the driver to take them to Madame Vitelle's establishment. Amanda had heard her aunt speak of this mantua-maker as being the best as well as the most expensive in Town. She knew that her

118

cousin, Rose, would have liked to employ Madame Vitelle herself but Lady Devine's plans for her daughter's glittering come-out did not stretch to patronising the mantua-maker.

"My mother was a French seamstress," Lady Glendarvon volunteered as they arrived at their destination, "and I have kept in contact with many of the *émigrés* who settled in London. Poor Madame Vitelle's family were noble when they were in France, but they lost everything in the Revolution."

"Your family must have been noble too," Amanda told her and was rewarded with a smile.

"I do not have a drop of noble blood in my veins but I am heartily glad that my daughter does."

By this time Lady Veronica was beginning to become restless and Lady Glendarvon instructed the driver to take her home and return for them with the carriage.

"When we are done with the seamstress and the milliner then it will be time for a ride in the Park where you will be seen by all."

Amanda wanted to tell her that she was not ready for that as yet, but she knew better than to oppose Lady Glendarvon's plans for her.

At the fashionable hour the paths of Hyde Park were thronged with fine carriages, splendid horses and modishly dressed people, some of them on foot. Because there were so many people and carriages crowding the narrow paths it was necessary to travel at a very sedate pace which made it easier to see and be seen, except for a few young bucks eager to show off their driving skill to impressionable young ladies.

Lady Glendarvon nodded affably towards almost every carriage, pointing out their passengers to her protégée. "Many of these people will be at your ball, Amanda."

"Oh, surely it isn't necessary to go to such trouble and expense, my lady."

"It is impossible to launch you properly without, even if you are presented at court."

"You are taking a prodigious amount of trouble over this."

"It is necessary for me to take a deal of trouble about everything I do. Since my marriage the *ton* have been awaiting me to stumble. I have not as yet and have no intention of doing so."

Amanda sank back into the squabs. "That is all very well but I am past the age of débutante. Moreover, I have not the looks to attract the kind of match you envisage and I am bound to tell you if I ever do marry it will be only for love."

"I would not wish you to do anything else. You may have already heard a good deal of tattle about me around the Town and it is no secret I danced at the Opera House before my marriage. My late husband was much older than I, but I can assure you I would not have contemplated matrimony if I had not harboured a definite fondness in my heart for him."

"Knowing you as I have come to do, my lady, I did not doubt it for one moment."

Lady Glendarvon cast her a grateful smile. "As for your age it is of no real account. Lots of girls do not come-out when they are supposed for all manner of reasons; health, bereavement, even financial. It cannot matter, for most gentlemen in search of a bride are considerably older than any débutante, and if you regard your appearance as a bar I can only conclude you have not lately glanced in your mirror. When Glendarvon returns from Newmarket he will be most pleasantly surprised by the change in you."

"Do you suppose he will notice, ma'am?" Amanda couldn't help but retort, and then immediately regretted her hasty words.

"There are two matters on which my stepson is a nonpareil, my dear. One is his judgement of horseflesh, and the other his eye for females. Oh goodness, you must brace yourself, Miss Westwood. Lady Devine and her daughter are approaching."

Amanda found that her heart began to beat fast as her aunt's carriage came towards them. Lady Devine raised her quizzing glass and stared just as Lady Glendarvon instructed the driver to slow down almost to a walking pace so that they could be seen the better. Amanda smiled a tentative greeting to her relatives but Lady Devine simply stared as her carriage passed theirs without slowing down in the least. Rose merely turned away in a deliberate manner.

"They have cut me," Amanda said in astonishment. "I could not conceive that they would do so."

"They will come around before long," Lady Glendarvon assured her. "They will not want to miss your ball and they will be obliged to acknowledge you then. Besides, your aunt would not wish to cause any undue tattle. She is fond of exchanging *on-dits* but I doubt if she would like to feature in one."

Rose turned around once the carriages had passed one another and glared at the departing one. "Mama, did you see that splendid hat?"

"Lady Glendarvon always did have style," her mother answered grudgingly.

"Not Lady Glendarvon. Amanda. Lady Glendarvon must have taken her in hand and she looks ... quite splendid. Oh, Mama, it is not to be borne. She will entirely overshadow my come-out. We are cousins and there are bound to be comparisons."

"Stuff and nonsense, my dear. Her appearance may be tolerable but it is nothing out of the ordinary. Corn-coloured hair and such vividly blue eys are quite outmoded now. Indeed she is positively vapid. Mrs. Bosomworth agrees with me upon that score. You can be certain your cousin will not make a brilliant match despite her portion or Lady Glendarvon's patronage. You are far more handsome, not to mention affable in your manner. Amanda has such a tart tongue no gentleman is like to be left in doubt of it for very long."

"Lady Glendarvon's patronage is no trifle, Mama. You were anxious enough to secure it for me. I have heard say the Prince of Wales is to be a guest at Amanda's ball."

"That is only because the old lecher has designs on Lady Glendarvon despite being currently involved with Lady Hertford. Do not worry your head, my dear. We shall have an influential crowd at *your* ball, as well as an army of suiters. Just look at Julia Simpkins' bonnet, Rose. Have you ever seen anything so hideous? What can she be thinking of?"

"Do you suppose Amanda has set her cap at Lord Glendarvon?"

Lady Devine laughed. "My dear, what a ludicrous suggestion. She loathes him for what he did to her father, and quite rightly too. The man is a rake and not to be trusted by any young lady."

Rose was taken aback. "But when you thought he was about to offer for me you were quite overcome with delight."

"Faddle, Rose. What nonsense you speak."

"He is devilishly handsome."

"He has always been appreciative of you, dear. No, I assure you Amanda is not to Lord Glendarvon's taste. Mrs. Roehampton is more to his style. He is often to be found in her company, I am told."

"A Cyprian," Rose murmured. "Gentlemen do not wed Cyprians, Mama."

"His father did."

"Lady Glendarvon was an opera dancer, which I think is quite different, much as I hesitate to contradict you, Mama."

Lady Devine's long, aristocratic nose quivered with something very much akin to distaste. "To me it is the same. Hopkin drive us home. I am quite done-up, and being obliged to listen to your foolish prattle is no cure at all!"

When Amanda returned from Hyde Park she felt both sad and weary. It was true the Devines had displayed little affection towards her, but it remained that they were her only family and their attitude towards what must be considered good fortune was saddening. When Lady Glendarvon went to rest before dinner, Amanda returned to her room to the vexing problem of where to put all her books, but she had only just removed her bonnet and pelisse when a visitor was announced. With her heart racing she hurried back downstairs to find her brother and another gentleman ensconced in the drawing-room.

"Cedric, dearest," she greeted him her hands outstretched, "how good it is to see you again."

They embraced briefly before he said, "It is good to see you in such rude health, Manda. I was concerned for you and did call on several occasions while you were indisposed but Lady Glendarvon informed me you were not well enough to receive visitors on any of those occasions."

"As you can clearly see I am quite recovered."

"And you are looking most fetching too. I see Lady Glendarvon's hand in this." When Amanda glanced at the other person, a handsome young man with a dandified air, her brother said, "Manda, dear, allow me to introduce you to my very dear friend, Sir Hedley Flint."

Amanda curtseyed as the young man took her hand and raised it to his lips. "I am delighted to make your acquaintance, Sir Hedley," she murmured.

"And I yours, Miss Westwood," he replied, gazing deep into her eyes.

"My cousin, Miss Devine, has spoken of you in glowing terms," she told him moving away as soon as she was able.

Sir Hedley's eyebrows rose a little. "Indeed? How odd it is she has never spoken of you, something about which I am resolved to take her to task. I consider it a crime that you have been hidden from sight for so long. What a loss that has been for Society and it is as well that is being remedied with no further delay."

As Amanda's cheeks grew pink under his admiring scrutiny, Sir Cedric said, "As you will deduce, my dear, Flinty is a tongue-pad." Amanda laughed, albeit uncomfortably as her brother went on, "I cannot tell you how relieved I am to see you beneath this roof, Manda. The news of your come-out is all over Town and everyone I speak to is in a fidge to make your acquaintance. This is the most deuced good fortune!"

His sister was more guarded in her enthusiasm. "I do trust it will turn out to be so."

"It can be no other," Sir Hedley points out.

"You cannot wish to stay in Sir Gile's household," Sir Cedric chided.

"I am now in Lord Glendarvon's household," she pointed out.

"In any event you will no longer be obliged to run to and fro at Aunt Ambrosia's bidding, or teaching misses to dance a cotillion. I for one am delighted you are getting your due."

"If my due is becoming prey to fortune hunters," Amanda pointed out.

"No man of the least sensibility would pursue you on account of your fortune, Miss Westwood," Sir Hedley told her, in such earnestness Amanda blushed again.

"Flinty is correct," Sir Cedric affirmed. "You are an uncommonly handsome woman, Manda. Moreover, I am persuaded you must have come to realise at last that Glendarvon has a heart after all."

"Oh no, Cedric. I cannot agree with you upon that point. Pride in excess I grant you and an overweening sense of propriety, but I cannot concede, in all truthfulness, that he has a heart."

"At least he has a string of fine racehorses," Sir Hedley said with a laugh causing Amanda to look at him curiously.

Sir Cedric looked a trifle uncomfortable but a moment later went on to explain without meeting Amanda's searching gaze, "Flinty and I are just back from Newmarket. All but one of Glendarvon's fillies won their races to our mutual benefit, might I add."

Amanda's curious look turned to one of dismay. "Cedric, how can you bear to wager on horses? You could have lost your entire allowance."

"But I did not. Quite the contrary in fact."

"Well, I confess I am as cross as two sticks about the entire matter."

"Oh, don't be such a prosy bore," he scoffed,

straightening his buff-coloured waistcoat. "You have taken against gaming even when it is only on a small scale."

"Do you wonder?"

"To be all the crack in this Town one needs to place a wager now and again, and do recall that there are winners as well as losers. Glendarvon invariably wins as you well know."

"Do not I beg of you use Lord Glendarvon as a model of behaviour. You will end up in dun territory if you do."

"And you are fast becoming a scold, something I do not like to see in you, Manda," her brother retorted.

"I implore you to be prudent."

"You may be assured, Miss Westwood," Sir Hedley told her, "I will endeavor to curb Sir Cedric's excesses."

Sir Cedric laughed. "Only when you are able to control your own, Flinty, but," he added, addressing himself to his sister once more, "you must rest assured, my dear, I shall not be dished up by my gaming."

"I trust that you will not for it is several years before Lady Veronica is of marriageable age, so you will be obliged to contrive until then."

Both gentlemen laughed this time. "That minx has confided in you, I note," Sir Cedric said at last. "It might not be as ludicrous as you evidently believe. After all, Lady Veronica will come-out just when I am of an age when most gentlemen wish to become leg-shackled."

"At an age when most gentlemen have run

through their own fortunes, more like," she retorted.

"I have no fortune, merely a small allowance which scarce covers my expenses."

"Then it is not like that Glendarvon will accept an offer from you for his precious half-sister however long you wait," Amanda told him, a hint of sisterly malice in her voice.

"Well, if all I am to receive is a set-down, I shall take myself off to more convivial company."

"Do not allow me to drive you away with my waspish tongue," Amanda begged in a plaintive tone.

"You need not fear that," Sir Hedley assured her. "Your brother merely gammons you, for we are already engaged to dine elsewhere, but I shall make sure you see us again soon, Miss Westwood, if only for my own sake."

"You are too kind," she responded, although her mind was still troubled.

They took their leave of her and just as she was about to go upstairs again Lady Veronica came hurrying down the stairs, her face a picture of dismay.

"I saw Sir Cedric leaving the house. I am certain it was he."

"He made only a short visit. He was merely enquiring after my health."

"It is too bad. How could he call here and not insist upon seeing me?"

"I do not doubt he will call upon you and Lady Glendarvon when he has more time to devote to you."

Not to be mollified the little girl turned on

her heel and ran up the stairs, watched by
Amanda. She was just about to pursue her
when she heard a carriage stop outside the
mansion. A moment later the marquis strode
into the hall, stripping off his gloves which he
threw into his hat and handed to the footman.
When he caught sight of Amanda he looked
startled.

"Miss Westwood, you look much improved
since our last encounter."

The reminder of the last time she had seen
him was not welcome but she contrived to answer, "I thank you, my lord."

As the house-steward took the marquis's
coat he subjected her to more of that disconcerting scrutiny. "I am bound to confess, Miss
Westwood, you have become quite ravishing
since my stepmother has taken you in hand."
His face relaxed into an unexpected smile
which disconcerted her anew. "Let me hasten
to add the basic material could not have been
better."

"I am quite overcome by such flattery, my
lord," she responded, not troubling to hide her
sarcasm.

He was not put out and continued to smile
at her. "I am fully aware that no amount of
flummery on my part is like to turn your
head."

"Not mine, perchance, but there are those
who are more easily influenced." At her curt
tone he frowned. "You have just returned from
Newmarket, I understand."

All at once he looked well-pleased with himself, something which did nothing to curb

Amanda's resentment. "A most satisfactory sojourn, Miss Westwood."

"So my brother informs me," she responded and he could not miss the ice dripping from her tongue any longer. "On this occasion it has been satisfactory for him too, but I fear it will not always be so if he seeks to emulate those with far more means. In my opinion such a course can only lead to total disaster."

A cool look came over the marquis's face and Amanda knew it was prudent to exhibit caution before taking him to task. However, fear for her brother made her a trifle reckless.

"What a gloomy picture you paint, Miss Westwood, but I would appreciate it if you would be plain with me. What is your exact grievance, if indeed there is only the one?"

Ignoring his sarcasm she found the courage to look him directly in the face. "You would oblige me by discouraging my brother from gaming."

The marquis drew a sigh. "I regret, Miss Westwood, any attempt to discourage what is a very natural urge in any young man would meet with failure. In any event Sir Cedric does not game above the normal."

"I find your indifference disturbing, my lord, especially as my brother looks upon you as someone to be emulated. Your tailor, your habits, everything about you represents the ultimate in all that is to be desired in a gentleman."

"You evidently find that distasteful, and I can only regret it. Be assured, Sir Cedric will find his own identity in due course."

"Let us hope it is not too late."

Amanda started up the stairs, knowing that to continue this conversation would only lead to even more bad feeling then there already was, but it was soon evident he had no intention of letting her off so easily.

"Too late for what, Miss Westwood?" When she made no reply he went on. "What really concerns you is that Cedric looks to me rather than you for any counsel, not any fears for his financial well-being. I sincerely regret that your stubborn prejudice blinds you to the fact that I would do nothing to compromise his future. On the contrary I hope to guide him away from the more dissolute ways of youth, but I shall do it in my own way, not yours, which is like to pitch him further into scapegrace behaviour."

"Your own behaviour, my lord, renders you utterly unfit to guide any young person."

His face twisted into a mask of anger. "You termagant. It is no wonder your relatives were glad to be done with you."

By this time Amanda was close to tears. She was trembling too, not intending to allow the matter to degenerate into a duel of words between them. However, it was certainly true that she had a quick temper and a sharp tongue. Mayhap, her aunt and uncle were right to be done with her.

"In all probability you will not be obliged to suffer me under your roof for much longer, my lord, for my portion is certain to attract any number of suitors."

She lifted her skirts and hurried up the

stairs, relieved when he remained in the hall below.

"By gad I pray that is so," he called after her, "for I shall never be more grateful for anything!"

NINE

It was to be a very special evening at the Theatre Royal, Drury Lane. George Frederick Cooke and Sarah Siddons were to appear in a version of *The Gamester*, and even though it was a thorny subject close to Amanda's heart she did, nevertheless, look forward to seeing the country's foremost actor and actress. So, it appeared, did most of the *beau monde*, for the theatre was filled to capacity.

Prominently seated in Lord Glendarvon's box, Amanda was beginning to appreciate how much more pleasant was this situation of privilege compared to the one she had been obliged to endure for the last few years. It had been surprisingly easy for her to slip into a life of privilege once again, as opposed to the role of subservience she had believed hers for ever more. Being befriended by someone like Lady Glendarvon would have been enough for Amanda, but a nagging voice inside her insisted upon reminding her frequently that her new comfortable existence was mainly due to the marquis's largesse.

Before they left for the theatre, Amanda had surveyed herself in the mirror which, such a short time ago, caused her such anguish. Now she could scarcely recognise the modish girl in pink satin with her mother's diamond necklace at her throat and fine feathers in her hair. The reflection in the mirror bore no resemblance to the dowdy female who had taught such a short time ago at Miss Millbeck's Academy for Young Ladies.

Nowadays whenever she and Lady Glendarvon ventured out they were often accosted by ladies of the *ton* eager to introduce Amanda to their bachelor sons. One frequent caller at Glendarvon House was Sir Hedley Flint. He no longer waited to accompany Sir Cedric whenever he came to see his sister; Sir Hedley called in often on his own account. Amanda found Sir Hedley amusing and didn't wonder Rose Devine had set her cap at him.

While that part of her social life was quite satisfactory, Amanda still felt uncomfortable whenever she thought about Lord Glendarvon. Since their angry exchange a few days earlier she had not spoken to him, although she had often caught sight of him entering or leaving the house, but she considered it prudent to stay out of his way as much as possible. It was evident they were never going to enjoy any degree of cordiality, and something deep inside her derived a good deal of satisfaction from that knowledge. She didn't want to be taken in by his excess of charm, as she had witnessed happen in so many other females. Amanda suspected it would be easy for her too to succumb, if only she allowed herself to forget her extreme prejudice against him, but that was something she was determined never to do.

"Do look, Amanda," the marchioness was saying, indicating with her lace fan to the opposite side of the theatre. "His Royal Highness, The Duke of Kent, with Madame Saint Laurent."

The portly duke was acknowledging the acclaim of the crowd as he settled into his box, his mistress at his side.

"Why are the princes such a rackety crowd!" Amanda asked.

"They are no different to any other men, for all that they are royal," Lady Glendarvon explained. "They enjoy their pleasures as do we lesser mortals. However, I suppose it is true to say they like them rather better. In any event Madame Saint Laurent would not be acceptable as a royal princess. I don't doubt that the duke would marry her if he could. I pity him a little, for it is a shame that they cannot enjoy married happiness. My own marriage, which was much frowned upon in some quarters, short as it was, had been sublimely happy."

Amanda drew her eager gaze away from the other playgoers and looked at her mentor. "It warms my heart to hear you say so, my lady, but so many matches are not so happy."

"Often marriages are contracted for dynastic reasons which can lead to a deal of unhappiness. Whatever the temptations, my dear, I do trust you will not marry for position alone."

Amanda felt her cheeks growing pink. "Indeed not, my lady." After a moment, she ventured, "It is strange that Lord Glendarvon has not married."

"Not as yet," his stepmother amended. "It is no secret that his lordship is notoriously difficult to please." Amanda laughed knowingly. "As a very young man he declared, very sweetly I own, that he would not wed until he found a female to make him as happy as I did his father. Let me add that young Glendarvon is not so easily pleased as his father," she added with a laugh and then, "Ah, Sir Giles and Lady Devine have arrived."

"I wonder if they will cut me again," Amanda mused, glancing in the direction of their box where her aunt was fussily arranging everyone in their seats.

"It would be foolish of them to do so. After your come-out ball, Amanda, it is evident you are going to be all the crack in this Town, and if they choose to set their faces against you it will only start the tongues clacking. I do not think Lady Devine would be so foolish to allow that, especially as it is in my power to bar Miss Devine from Almacks."

Amanda shot her a curious glance. "You would not be so hard-hearted, my lady."

"They have always sought to injure you."

"I would not want Rose to be humiliated in that way," Amanda protested just as Sir Giles bowed stiffly in their direction.

Lady Glendarvon and Amanda inclined their heads in acknowledgement and Lady Devine nodded unsmilingly, no doubt aware that many eyes would witness her every move.

Rose, however, continued to remain aloof, refusing to acknowledge her cousin.

"Miss Devine has so much," Lady Glendarvon pointed out. " 'Tis such a pity she cannot be more charitable towards you."

"Envy is a cruel affliction," Amanda agreed. "Although why she should envy me I cannot conceive."

"That is easy for someone with two eyes to ascertain."

Amanda sighed. "I pray I shall never suffer its pains."

Lady Glendarvon put one hand on Amanda's. "My dear, you have far too generous a spirit to be afflicted in that manner."

Amanda looked abashed at such praise. "You attribute me with nobler qualities than I possess. If I were the creature you believe me to be I would find it easier to be grateful to Lord Glendarvon for his generosity towards me and my brother."

"He does not seek any gratitude, my dear." She began to smile and wave towards the pit where a number of gentlemen were jostling for a seat.

Amanda's entire demeanour began to brighten when she saw Sir Cedric and she smiled broadly when she caught sight of Sir Hedley Flint as he bowed low towards their box. The gentlemen looked so handsome in their evening dress and not for the first time Amanda wondered if there was one among them to whom she could lose her heart completely.

"What a crush there is here tonight," Lady

Glendarvon murmured. "The start cannot now be far away."

"I am content enough to watch everyone else arriving. Everyone looks so splendid."

"You look no less handsome yourself, my dear. Many people have commented upon it to me, and tonight you are drawing many admiring glances."

"It is kind of them but I would not for anything wish to outshine my cousin."

"Resign yourself that you already do. It is not a deliberate act, for she is a pretty chit and tolerably well-dressed, but you are by far the more handsome, hence Lady Devine's ire."

"This Season means so much to her, my lady."

"I'll vouch that when you have achieved your heart's desire and made a brilliant match you will be bound to own how much it has meant to you too."

"A match of any description is exceeding difficult to envisage, my lady, for as I grew up in Aylsford I resigned myself to being an old maid."

Lady Glendarvon laughed delightedly. "That fate is most certainly not to be yours, my dear."

"It remains that I find it difficult to adjust to the possibility of a marriage, and an elevated one too."

"Your presence in Town has already excited a good deal of interest among the young bucks of the *ton*. It is obvious to me that Sir Hedley Flint, for one, is entranced by you."

"That is another vexation for me, ma'am.

You see, my cousin has set her cap at him and when I first came to Town I was given to believe her feelings were reciprocated."

"Do not trouble your head about Miss Devine. Bucks like Sir Hedley Flint always dangle after the greatest fortune. Oh, he is charming, I own, but there will be others of a more genuine heart who will wish to pay court to you. Every year at this particular time I am inundated by invitations to all the most prestigious assemblies, but this year it has become an avalanche and I can only assume that is due to your presence in my house. Everyone is in a fidge to make your acquaintance."

As always Amanda paid the greatest attention to everything Lady Glendarvon had to say to her, but all at once her interest was diverted by the sight of the marquis leading the most gorgeous creature into one of the boxes near theirs. Lady Glendarvon caught sight of him at almost the same time and she smiled, inclining her head in their direction. Amanda began to fan her cheeks furiously, unable to understand why his unexpected appearance had had this strange effect upon her, except that after their angry exchange she dreaded to see him again. Here in the relative safety of the theatre she was still disconcerted. He bowed stiffly in their direction, smiling ironically when he looked at Amanda, and then he returned his attention to the lady at his side. Amanda noted that he took a good deal of trouble to see that she was comfortably seated. Indeed, it was strange for her to witness him being so attentive to a lady other than the marchioness.

Amanda acknowledged that he never ventured out without looking immaculate, but she had never before seen him in evening dress. The dark blue evening coat contrasted with the snowy whiteness of his shirt and neckcloth, all of which suited admirably his dark looks. His companion in a high-waisted gown of dark blue velvet looked ravishing and was exciting a good deal of interest in the theater.

"Who is she?" Amanda could not help but ask.

"Mrs. Roehampton."

"A married lady?" Amanda was surprised. "Indeed no. She is bound to be a widow."

"Married, widowed, maiden, who knows? No, not, I think, a maiden lady," Lady Glendarvon added, smiling wryly.

All at once Amanda looked shocked. "You cannot mean she is . . . a Cyprian?"

"Yes indeed, she is, my dear, and one who is most popular with the gentlemen of the *beau monde*. Mrs. Roehampton is one who is able to pick and choose upon who she bestows her favours."

"Even so I would not have thought Lord Glendarvon would accompany her to the theatre."

"It is her box. Did you think such creatures were old crones who never left the area of Covent Garden? I had no notion you were so naive. I'll warrant Miss Devine is not."

When they glanced across to the Devine's box it could be seen that Rose was doing her utmost to attract the marquis's attention, but he had eyes for no one other than Mrs. Roehampton.

"Miss Devine did not grow up at Aylsford," Amanda murmured, swishing her fan to and fro in an agitated manner.

"Well-educated as you have been it appears there are a few omissions. There are many demi-reps in the Town," Lady Glendarvon went on to tell her, "who can afford to live in as great style as their illustrious patrons."

"Lord Glendarvon would not marry such a creature, would he?" Amanda asked in shocked tones.

"It is not unheard of for a man in his situation to do so, but I am confident Glendarvon will not. He has such a strong sense of lineage. I am beginning to despair of his ever finding a bride he deems worthy of his name."

It was a great relief to Amanda when the start of the drama brought the discomforting conversation to an end. Fortunately the acting talents of Mrs. Siddons and Mr. Cooke were sufficient to divert her mind, although on several occasions her glance did stray to the Cyprian's box until Lord Glendarvon became aware of her scutiny and she was obliged to look away.

At the start of the interval Amanda was obliged to acknowledge to herself that such entertainments exceeded anything she had experienced at Aylsford. The social life in London was far more congenial to her than she could ever have imagined. If only she could be less concerned about her family's hostility, the imminent publication of *The Terrors of Lucifer*, and most of all the proximity of Lord Glendarvon, life might have been perfect.

When the interval began Amanda remained in the box with Lady Glendarvon, knowing they were likely to receive many visitors before the entertainment recommenced. First into the box was a handsome and distinguished gentleman whom the marchioness introduced as the Duke of Rokesby. He expressed a lively interest in Amanda and although he was not to be considered a young man she thought he might be paying court to her but before long it became very evident that he was entranced by Lady Glendarvon.

Close on the Duke of Rokesby's heels came Sir Cedric and Sir Hedley Flint. "Is it not the most splendid play?" Amanda asked of them, leaving Lady Glendarvon to receive the duke's sole attention.

"It cannot possibly compare with the splendid good fortune of seeing you here, Miss Westwood," Sir Hedley declared.

"Such flummery," she responded, fluttering her fan.

Coquettishness came to her naturally Amanda had discovered, and she did not take excessive and, no doubt, insincere, flattery amiss.

"I see that you have rumbled my friend for the tongue-pad he is," Sir Cedric told her, laughing delightedly.

"I am no tongue-pad," the young man protested. "I am in earnest. The tattle is, Miss

Westwood, that your come-out ball is to be the most glittering of this Season."

"You need not doubt Lady Glendarvon's ability to arrange a splendid diversion," she confirmed.

"Nor your ability to sparkle more brightly than any star in the heavens," the baronet responded.

"Confound it, Flinty, you do go on a bit," Sir Cedric complained. "There's no need to prove that your tongue's well-hung. No one can be in any doubt of it."

"Tush, Cedric," his sister scolded. "You would find fault with a fat goose."

They all laughed although Amanda was aware that Lady Glendarvon was casting them concerned looks. It seemed evident that the marchioness did not approve of Sir Hedley as a suitor. It remained that Amanda found him amusing while not taking him in the least seriously.

Amidst all the laughter and conversation Amanda glanced across the auditorium to see the marquis was now standing in the Devine's box, addressing himself earnestly to Rose who evidently had no difficulty responding to his charm. All at once he looked across at Amanda, their eyes meeting before he looked away, speaking once more to her cousin as if no one else in the world existed.

Several other people of Lady Glendarvon's acquaintance called to pay their respects during the long interval which was vital to the social intercourse, as essential a part of the evening as the play itself. Few came for the play's sake alone, despite the popularity of the actors.

"Let us be gone to pay our respects elsewhere before the second half begins," Sir Cedric suggested to his friend.

"There is nowhere else I would rather be save in the company of Miss Westwood."

"If you exhibit the desire to ignore your acquaintances, Sir Hedley, it only shows you to have a derelict sense of propriety," Amanda told him.

"Reproved, alas," he cried with mock despair. "Come, Westwood, let us go where we may be appreciated better."

They took an elaborate leave of the two ladies and Amanda was still smiling when the marquis stepped in. She thought she should have expected to see him there, but considered him engaged elsewhere. Her smile faded somewhat and she looked away, not knowing quite how to address him, for the memory of their last angry exchange remained with her very vividly.

He bowed to the duke who displayed not the least desire to visit other acquaintances, kissed his stepmother's hand and then turned to Amanda who was affecting to quiz the crowd with the utmost interest.

"Miss Westwood," he said, sitting down in the chair vacated by Sir Hedley, "how do you enjoy the play?"

His tone was polite, but bore no warmth which was better than she might have looked for, although she acknowledged he could always be expected to exhibit the utmost urbanity in public whatever his true feelings might be. Amanda had come to realise his nature could be likened to a murky pool, in which ripples could be seen but not its unplumbed depths.

"Exceeding well, I thank you," she replied, taking her cue from his manner. She glanced across to Mrs. Roehampton's box where the Cyprian was surrounded by several distinguished gentlemen, all vying for her attention. When she gave the marquis her attention again her tone was cool. "I do not doubt that *you* are enjoying the proceedings."

His manner lost none of its urbanity. In fact she fancied he almost smiled. "How could I not? It is an excellent drama, the actors are superb and the company I find myself in cannot be bettered. One can ask for no more. My observation of you, Miss Westwood, leads me to believe you are of a like mind."

"How flattering it is to know I am being observed by a gentleman who has so much of greater interest to occupy him close at hand."

"My dear Miss Westwood, how can I help but be interested in you? Your activities needs must be of the greatest concern to me, for this Season at least."

"How flattering that is to me," she responded coolly.

"Naturally, after this Season is over it is like your interests will concern the gentleman who wins your heart. Again my observations lead me to conclude there will be many contenders for that privilege." He began to get to his feet. "It appears the second half is about to begin."

He bowed low before her. "Enjoy the rest of the evening, Miss Westwood, for I know I shall."

He withdrew and the Duke of Rokesby left at the same time, the latter gentleman with rather less eagerness Amanda noted. A few moments later the marquis was settled once again next to Mrs. Roehampton to whom he addressed himself with evident delight if their laughter was anything by which to judge.

"Rokesby is a delightful reprobate," Lady Glendarvon confided, "but he does tend to monopolise my attention, although I am bound to confess I do not mind overmuch."

"I had noted his partiality."

"Glendarvon seemed to have a good deal to say to you," the marchioness remarked in a careless tone.

"I assure you it was nothing out of the ordinary," Amanda replied, unable to prevent a note of stiffness creeping into her voice.

Lady Glendarvon cast her a searching look and in an effort to escape it Amanda peered across the crowded theatre. The marquis met her startled gaze and inclined his head but not before she had noted the ironic curl of his lips. Looking away quickly Amanda's eyes met those of her cousin and Rose Devine gave her a look of pure hatred before turning away.

Amanda sighed deeply, something observed by the marchioness, and she was glad when the entertainment commenced again and not just because of the excellence of the performance.

TEN

As the day of Amanda's come-out ball fast approached, Lady Glendarvon became even more fastidious about supervising the arrangements, and on one occasion when she was so engaged Amanda took the opportunity of slipping away from Glendarvon House on an errand of her own.

Since her arrival in London and learning that Sir Cedric was resident in their old house in Mount Street, she had been longing to visit him and this being her first opportunity to do so she did not intend to waste it. Accompanied by one of the marquis's footmen she walked the short distance from Glendarvon House as the day was a fine one and she did not intend to be absent for long. She was fortunate in finding Sir Cedric at home with a number of his cronies keeping him company.

As she stepped into the once familiar hall a host of memories assailed her. Recollection of her parents, clad in velvet and silks on their way to a rout or a masquerade, the memory of

Sir Nigel arriving home roaring drunk after a night with his cronies.

"Manda, what do you think of the old place?" Sir Cedric asked as he came down the stairs towards her, looking very much the master of the house, something which brought a lump to her throat.

It was immediately evident that the marquis had kept the house in excellent condition, far better, in fact, than when she and her family had lived there. "It looks wonderful," she answered truthfully. "and it warms my heart to see you here."

A number of Sir Cedric's friends followed him down the stairs, proclaiming their delight and good fortune in being there while she had called in.

"Miss Westwood," Sir Hedley cried. "What a most welcome surprise."

Sir Cedric grinned. "Flinty will be crying roast meat all day. Come along, Manda, let me show you around."

They wandered from room to room, followed by a noisy group of young gentlemen. "It is so good to see everything I believed lost to us," Amanda sighed as she ran her hand lovingly along her mother's spinet, recalling the hours she had spent herself mastering some expertise at the instrument. "He has disposed of nothing."

"Why not play for us?" one of the gentlemen invited.

She smiled. "No indeed, Captain Willis, not on this occasion. I must leave here very soon. There is no chaperone and I'm persuaded Lady

Glendarvon would not approve of my being here."

As they walked back down the stairs Sir Cedric said in a low voice, "You must own now, Manda, that Glendarvon is a good sort of a fellow after all."

Amanda sighed. "Cedric, I confess I no longer know what to think about him. He may be a villain or an angel. Time alone will tell the truth of the matter. Oh, Cedric, that is Mama's portrait."

She paused on the stairs to admire the Gainsborough painting of the late Lady Annabel Westwood, resplendent in a feathered hat and silk gown. Amanda hadn't set eyes on it for more than nine years and had never realised how beautiful her mother had been in her youth.

"It is splended, is it not?" Sir Hedley asked. "Lady Westwood bestowed her beauty upon you Miss Westwood. There can be no doubt about that."

"You are very kind to say so," she responded, her eyes misting with tears.

Amanda hadn't realised how moved she would be at the sight of their one-time possessions, complete and just how she remembered them from her childhood days. Her eyes were so misted she missed the last step and was only saved from falling by the quick action of Sir Hedley Flint who steadied her in his arms. It was at that very moment that the front door opened and the marquis strode in. The unexpectedness of his arrival caused Amanda to step back sharply from Sir Hedley's arms, for the marquis's face was a mask of fury.

"So this is why one of my footmen is standing outside. Am I correct in assuming you are here alone?"

"I called upon my brother," she stammered. "I had no notion anyone else would be here with him."

"I will escort you back home immediately. Come."

After issuing the peremptory order the marquis walked back towards the door. Amanda glanced helplessly at her brother and his friends, who all at once found their hessian boots of the greater interest. After a moment she followed Lord Glendarvon out of the house.

He was waiting at the side of his phaeton, slapping his riding whip against his boots and Amanda had the oddest feeling he would have liked to used it on her just then. He handed her up onto the box in a silence which persisted until they reached Park Lane. Amanda had never seen him so angry and it troubled her. Once, goading him to anger would have been a satisfying business, but on this occasion she was forced to acknowledge he had been correct in his censure of her.

When they arrived back at Glendarvon House he hurried to hand her down but she managed to climb down without his assistance. Just as she was about to go inside the house he said, "Miss Westwood," and when she paused he went on in the same icy tones, "in future you would oblige me by doing nothing more to betray Lady Glendarvon's trust in you."

"You insult me if you believe I would ever do anything to jeopardise that," she told him and then hurried inside before he could say anything more or become aware of the tears which now threatened to overcome her.

When the great day of the ball arrived the house was in a turmoil from the earliest hour. At the outset Amanda thought she would hate all the fuss and botheration involved, but although she still harboured a modicum of reserve she realised she was going to heartily enjoy being the object of everyone's attention. Unlike lady Devine, who left many of the arrangements for Rose's ball to Amanda's unaccustomed supervision, Lady Glendarvon had gleefully set about planning a most superb diversion.

At the time she had written the invitations in her excellent hand she had found her quill trembling at some of the illustrious names on the list. She continued to keep up a regular correspondence with Lucy, imagining, as she wrote, her friend's amusement at the pen-portraits of the important people she met. Lucy responded with questions about Lord Glendarvon about whom Amanda was somehow reluctant to write. Lucy also looked forward to the day when *The Terrors of Lucifer* was published at last. Amanda dreaded it. In fact she did everything possible to cast all thoughts of it from her mind. If she had ever suspected it would be published one day she would have destroyed it long ago, but she appreciated it was now far too late for regrets. When the day finally arrived Amanda knew she would be obliged to pretend as never before, for she was determined it would never be known as she was the author of such a silly piece of work.

It did not surprise Amanda that Lady Glendarvon thought so highly of her maid, Nel. Not only was the marchioness always impeccably turned out, but the maid had effected quite a change in her too. Whenever she ventured forth now her gown was of the very latest design, her hats drawing the envy of many and her hair a clever confection of natural curls which bore no resemblance to that severe style she used to favour. Amanda fancied that Lucy and all the others at Aylsford would not recognise her now.

When the time came for her to dress for the ball, she had just begun, watched by Lady Veronica, when there came a knock on the door. When Nel came in she told her, "Her ladyship has charged me to assist you, Miss Westwood."

"Lady Glendarvon will require your services herself," Amanda responded.

"Her Ladyship is already dressed and gone downstairs, ma'am."

Lady Veronica watched as Nel assisted Amanda, occasionally inspecting the gown which had been put out by the young maid assigned to her.

"If only I were old enough to attend," the girl sighed.

"Your turn will come soon enough," Amanda responded.

"It cannot be soon enough for me. Did you know that the Prince Regent has promised to attend?"

Amanda shivered slightly. "I cannot conceive how your mama has contrived it."

"His Royal Highness has a fondness for Mama, so 'tis simple. He makes no secret of his feelings for her as you will observe. It must be exceeding vexing for Lady Hertford."

"I'm persuaded Lady Hertford has no real cause to fret, for your mama is too full of good sense even to contemplate becoming his . . ."

"Chère amie?" the girl supplied, totally unabashed. "I dare say you are correct. You may be more interested to see Lord Byron who has intimated his intention to attend. No doubt when he speaks to you—if indeed he does—you will be as mute as a fish. Most people are in awe of him."

The thought of actually meeting the famous poet was so exciting to Amanda Nel was driven to implore, "Do stay still, ma'am."

"Mama has given me permission to watch the guests arriving from the upper landing, but it will be a great temptation to come down to see everyone at closer quarters."

"You must resist that temptation," Amanda told her laughingly, "otherwise your mama will be very angry."

"I don't see why I should resist temptation; no one else appears to do so."

Again Amanda laughed, unable to argue on the veracity of that statement.

"There, ma'am, I think you will do," Nel declared, putting the last touches to Amanda's hair and clipping a pearl necklace at her throat.

Amanda jumped to her feet and pirouetted for the benefit of all those in the room, including her own young maidservant who had been watching Nel's expertise in silent amazement.

"Well, what do you think, Lady Veronica?"

The child appeared pensive for a moment or two and then said, "Tolerable, Miss Westwood, tolerable."

"That is praise indeed, Miss Westwood," Nel assured her.

"Evidently the Glendarvon's streak is very strong in you, Lady Veronica," Amanda told her laughingly. "Now, off you go to your supper child."

The girl walked with her to the door. "Oh indeed. My nursery supper," she said contemptuously. "I shall be obliged to be content with that while you enjoy a splendid dinner downstairs with Sir Cedric."

Lady Veronica made her way back to the nursery while Amanda went downstairs to the drawing-room. The servants were all on duty tonight, every one of the footmen splendidly attired in scarlet and gold livery. The footman on duty outside the drawing-room sprang to attention as she approached and hastened to open the door for her. From within she could hear the sound of laughter and conversation, for Lady Glendarvon had invited a number of intimates to the dinner which preceded the ball.

More than ever aware that on this particular occasion she was going to be the centre of everyone's attention, all at once Amanda found the notion unbearable. She surely could not live up to such high expectations of her. A social success, a brilliant marriage—it could not possibly be hers, not when so many others had been brought up to the task.

For a few short moments Amanda was tempted to turn on her heel and run as far away as possible, but as the door was opened she heard Lady Glendarvon say, "This must be Miss Westwood at last."

The door was thrust open before her and realising flight was impossible, Amanda took a deep breath before stepping inside. The chatter in the room abruptly ceased. Lady Glendarvon smiled with pleasure as her eyes alighted on her protégée. Sir Cedric stared at his sister in astonishment, Sir Hedley Flint in admiration, and the marquis raised his quizzing glass to observe her much as he had done on that day at her uncle's house.

"My dear you look, quite, quite ravishing," declared the Countess of Derringham, an old acquaintance of the marchioness.

The idea for the gown had been Lady Glendarvon's and Amanda had to admit to herself the silver cloth beneath a diaphanous overskirt of white gauze had been pure inspiration, for the material shimmered with every movement she made. With her mother's pearls at her neck, wrist and one of Lady Glendarvon's dainty diadems nestling in her curls, on this evening at least, Amanda could at least feel equal to any of the beauties of the *beau monde*.

"Manda," Sir Cedric cried when he turned to look at her, "you look so fetching I scarce recognised you as m'sister."

The others laughed as she dropped into a deep curtsey before them.

The marquis allowed his quizzing glass to drop at last before he came towards her. "Westwood, you will never win favour in a lady's eyes with such ungallant remarks."

Sir Cedric looked bewildered, genuinely not understanding his *faux pas*.

"Too true!" opined Sir Hedley. "Westwood has more hair than wit to insinuate Miss Westwood is ever anything but delightful in the extreme."

The marquis cast the young man a wry look. "No one could ever accuse you of being ungracious, sir."

Before anyone else could reach her the marquis bowed low before her. "Miss Westwood, allow me the pleasure of talking you into dinner."

Again she curtseyed. "I am honoured by your condescention, my lord."

He cast her a wry look and it was clear that his anger was no more. Amanda could not help but be glad of it. She took his proffered arm and led the way into the dining-room where a footman stood behind every chair.

The marquis sat at the head of the table almost beneath the painting of his late father whom he resembled so much. Amanda didn't wonder Lady Glendarvon held him in such high esteem; every time she set eyes on him she must be reminded of her late husband.

Amanda found herself seated at one side of

the marquis while his stepmother sat at the other. A prodigious array of fine porcelain dishes was set on the table containing a selection of fish, meat and fowl with accompanying vegetables. Lady Glendarvon employed an excellent kitchen staff, but despite the splendour of the food before her, Amanda found she had very little appetite. She was far too excited to eat. Besides whenever she attempted to take a morsel someone began to engage her in conversation.

"Every time I find myself in the company of His Royal Highness," began one lady, "I wonder if Lady Hertford will still be in favour."

Lady Glendarvon merely smiled while the Duke of Rokesby replied, "I wonder of the Princess of Wales will *ever* be in favour," a remark which caused the rest of them much merriment.

"Miss Westwood," Lady Patton confided across the table as the laughter died away, "do you read?"

"Indeed I do, ma'am," Amanda replied, anticipating a discussion on Lord Byron's works, for his name was on everyone's lips nowadays. "Poetry is a particular favourite."

"I am more addicted to novels, I must confess. In fact I have today received a new one on the very day of its publication, and I am in a fidge to read it. Hatchards expect it to become all the crack."

"What is the title?" Lady Glendarvon enquired.

"*The Terrors of Lucifer.* Does that not sound utterly delicious?"

The accommodating smile Amanda had been affecting throughout the meal froze on her lips. Feeling stupid she found she was unable to say anything. Indeed there was nothing she could say on the subject.

Fortunately Lady Glendarvon's interest saved her having to trouble. "It sounds to be a Gothic. I must instruct Mr. Scott and the circulating library to save me a copy. I am a trifle addicted to such stories. Amanda, we must go on the morrow."

Suddenly Amanda was aware of the marquis's sardonic gaze. They knew! she decided, panicking inwardly. They all knew she was the author!

"You appear terrorised before you even read it," he told her.

"Tush," his stepmother chided. "Can you not see that this evening is an ordeal for her?"

"You need not worry, Miss Westwood," he assured her. "Lady Glendarvon and I will be at your side."

She managed to respond with a nervous smile. How could they possibly know? she told herself, regretting her momentary panic. She realised that she would have to refrain from flying into a pucker every time the novel was mentioned if she had any hope of remaining anonymous.

"Miss Westwood, you are not eating," Sir Hedley declared after a while.

"Is it any wonder?" she answered, laughing nervously. "I have never been in such a fidge in all my life!"

"You really have no cause for such concern," Lady Glendarvon told her in a soothing tone. "You are bound to be a triumph."

"Hear, hear!" echoed Sir Hedley Flint.

"I'm deuced proud of you, m'dear," Sir Cedric admitted, drinking up his claret before allowing the footman to refill his glass to the brim.

"I hope you will still be proud of me when I step on everyone's toes during the dance," she retorted.

"I do trust you will not step on mine," the marquis told her, setting his wineglass back on the table. Amanda noted with some surprise that he refused a refill. "As I am obliged to stand up with you at the outset I should take that amiss."

"You are obliged to do no such thing," she retorted, her cheeks growing red.

"Let me assure you it will be a pleasure," he amended, something which caused her to blush to an even greater degree. "To that end I must insist that you eat in order to keep up your strength. You will be in much demand this evening and it would not do for you to swoon."

So saying he began to spoon small helpings of everything on to her plate. Before she could protest Sir Hedley claimed her attention once again.

"Miss Westwood no one would gainsay Lord Glendarvon's right in claiming you for the first set, but I do entreat you to save the very next one for me."

"It will be a pleasure, Sir Hedley," she responded.

"And another for me," Sir Cedric insisted.

"At this rate I shall have all the dances spoken for before we have even finished dinner."

"You must reserve one set for Prinny should he wish to stand up with you." Amanda looked alarmed at the prospect but Lady Derringham went on regardless. "Mayhap you should hope he does not, for he does present an outlandish figure since he became so stout. I recall a time when he was a mere slip of a fellow."

The others laughed, the Duke of Rokesby saying in his droll manner, "That was an unconscionable time ago."

"Have I heard correctly," another guest asked, "that the Russian ambassador will be present?"

"You have indeed," Lady Glendarvon replied, "and Count Lieven has been kind enough to supply me with a great Russian delicacy—caviare—which will be served at supper. It is, I assure you, quite delicious."

"Eat, Miss Westwood," the marquis hissed in her ear and Amanda was surprised when she discovered that she could after all manage a little.

However when she discovered she was the object of his lanquid gaze her appetite deserted her once more and she began to push to the food around with her fork.

"Does the prospect of this evening alarm you so much?" he asked a moment later. "I fancy your cousin, Miss Devine, will relish hers."

"As I said earlier, I am only alarmed at the very real prospect of standing on someone's toes. It would be dreadful if I were to tread on the Prince Regent's."

He looked amused. "Such faint-heartedness is most unlike you, Miss Westwood. I assure you that Prinny will not even notice if you do."

"Or mayhap Lord Byron. I have heard tell he is of a sullen disposition."

"That is most certainly true, but you must not allow that to trouble your head for Byron will not stand up with you tonight."

"If I am to stumble at all I just pray it will not be while *we* dance together, my lord." One dark eyebrow rose a little and she went on, "Having once inflicted damage upon your boot, I dare say scuffing your shoe would put me totally beyond the possibility of your forgiveness."

For a long moment he looked startled and then, throwing his head back, he began to roar with laughter while Amanda smiled grimly into her wineglass.

ELEVEN

When the time came to take their places at the head of the stairs to greet the guests, Amanda was truly terrified. Lady Glendarvon had contrived to invite the most important people in the land and Amanda felt she had a great responsibility to make the evening a success. However, learning that *The Terrors of Lucifer* was published could only adversely affect her nerves to a greater degree. That knowledge was constantly at the back of her mind. How she wished she had destroyed it long ago.

As they took their places Amanda caught sight of Lady Veronica darting around in the shadows. The girl put one finger to her lips and, chuckling to herself, Amanda turned away, affecting not to have seen her. However, the marquis had seen his sister and without a word to anyone turned around to hoist the protesting child onto one shoulder before taking her up the stairs.

"We are altogether too indulgent of that child," Lady Glendarvon confided.

162

"She is merely afflicted with the excitement of the evening, as we all are."

The marquis returned just then, straightening his coat. "Veronica has been warned in the strictest of terms she must not come down again. That child has the making of a hoyden, I fear."

His stepmother laughed. "I cannot envisage you administering any form of punishment on Veronica, and she knows that full well."

"Do not be so sure," he warned, and Amanda could not help but cast him a malicious smile.

"Lord Glendarvon dislikes spirit in girls of a tender age."

"I dislike it in females of any age," he countered, not to be outdone.

Carriages had begun to arrive and the footmen were stirring in the hall below. Amanda began to shiver slightly. The marquis glanced at her, asking, "Cold, Miss Westwood?" Before she could deny it he had adjusted her shawl, something which made her shiver all the more.

As the guests began to stream into Glendarvon House, Amanda's head swam with the effort it took to try and retain some memory of whom she had been presented to, and after a while her legs ached from so many curtseys.

"Here comes Brummel," the marquis whispered as the most elegant of gentlemen climbed the stairs towards them. "I did wonder if he would cry off in the end."

"We must contrive to keep him as far from Prinny as we can," Lady Glendarvon replied in a whisper.

"Why is that?" Amanda asked.

"Brummel and Prinny are no longer on speaking terms," the marchioness explained.

The last time they met they parted brass rags," the marquis added. "One does not insult His Royal Highness with impunity. Welcome, Brummel my dear fellow!"

Beau Brummel raised his quizzing glass to inspect the marquis. "By gad, Glendarvon, how dare you venture forth with your neckcloth so dishabille?"

Amanda looked at the marquis who wore an immaculately folded neckcloth and back to Brummel whose own did not look much different. To her surprise Lord Glendarvon laughed. "That is indeed a compliment from you, Brummel."

The famous dandy bowed before the two ladies and passed on to the ballroom. "How top-lofty he is, without possessing a drop of aristocratic blood in his veins!" Amanda exclaimed.

"You are exceeding honoured he has graced us with his presence this evening," Lady Glendarvon explained. "I can only think that this rift with Prinny causes him to solicit as much elevated company as he can contrive. Even now a gentleman's social standing can be made by a nod of his head."

"I consider him disagreeable."

"You are not obliged to like him," the marquis told her.

A moment later Beau Brummel was entirely forgotten when Amanda caught sight of her aunt, uncle and cousin arriving in the great hall of Glendarvon House. The marchioness put one hand on Amanda's shoulder. "See how Lady Devine appears to be quite out of humour," she pointed out and it appeared to be so. None of the Devines exhibited any of the excitement displayed by the other guests. "Moreover, Miss Devine seems to be in high dudgeon too."

"My lady, I do believe you are enjoying their discomfiture," Amanda responded.

Lady Glendarvon's eyes sparkled. "I am bound to confess I do dislike the kind of meanness of spirit exhibited by that woman."

She smiled warmly, however, when Amanda's relatives approached. "So kind of you to come," she murmured.

Lady Devine continued to look unhappy during the greetings and Rose remained positively hostile. "I am so glad you have honoured us with your presence," Amanda assured them.

"Your niece has a very good nature to say so, don't you think?" added the marquis.

The two ladies moved away but Sir Gile's cheeks grew red at the barb. "No one can doubt that my niece is the most fortunate creature to have been taken up by the likes of you, but if you hadn't ruined her father it would not have been necessary."

"Uncle Giles," Amanda snapped, "Lord Glendarvon is your host. Have you no thought of that?"

Sir Giles moved away and the marquis looked at Amanda in astonishment. "Can I have heard correctly? Miss Amanda Westwood leaping to *my* defence?"

In the face of his chiding Amanda immediately felt foolish and her cheeks grew pink. "I am persuaded you need no one to defend you, my lord," she retorted, "but I do have a thought for propriety and I regard it impudent for anyone to ride grub in your own establishment."

"That statement does not, I take it, apply to you," he retorted.

Amanda supposed she deserved that retort and replied, "Not on this evening in any event."

"I had no notion you were such a stickler for propriety," he persisted and she wished she hadn't spoken on his account. The marquis glanced past her to his stepmother. "Aylsford has instilled such virtues in Miss Westwood, Cecilia, mayhap we should consider it for Veronica in due course."

"Tush," came the marchioness's uncompromising reply. "Do not heed him, my dear. He is only gammoning you."

Amanda had no chance to feel vexed at his teasing, for it was then that the unmistakable figure of the Prince Regent entered the hall of Glendarvon House, accompanied by an equally voluptuous Lady Hertford, his current favorite. As they climbed the stairs, the Prince in the uniform of a Field Marshall, the garter star pinned to his breast, Amanda began to tremble once again.

She and Lady Glendarvon sank into deep curtseys while the marquis bowed low before their future king.

"Allow me to present Miss Amanda Westwood, Your Highness," the marquis invited.

"I recall your father well, m'dear," the Prince responded. "We gamed together often." Before Amanda was even out of her curtsey the Prince turned to the marchioness and took her hand in his podgy one. "My dear Lady Glendarvon, you are as handsome as ever."

"How kind you are to say so, sir, and how generous, for I know you are always surrounded by the fairest in the land."

Unaware of Lady Hertford's stony countenance the Prince went on, "That cannot possibly be so as long as you are missing from my retinue. Do tell me you will come more often to Carlton House."

"Whenever I am invited, sir. Tell me, how is Her Royal Highness?" she asked sweetly.

"Fair Cecilia, you know how to wound me. She is in rude health, more's the pity." He looked to the marquis then. "Well, Glendarvon, I don't believe I shall engage in gaming with you this evening." His look encompassed them all. "Glendarvon is always favoured by Lady Luck whenever we play at cards. I am determined that he shall not win my purse tonight."

When the Prince and his retinue passed into the ballroom Amanda said, "I cannot think that the Prince has anything to fear from playing cards with you, my lord."

"His pockets are always to let," answered the marquis.

"But he is the heir to the throne, the Regent

167

while the King suffers from lunacy. How can it be so?"

"Prinny is exceeding extravagant," Lady Glendarvon explained.

"There are few here tonight who are not."

"The Prince is more so."

All at once Amanda looked at the marquis and began to laugh. He was, understandably, bewildered by her mirth. "Do you find his situation so amusing, Miss Westwood? I declare you do not in your own close relatives."

" 'Twas only a thought that occurred to me," she gasped.

"Do let us share in it if it is so amusing," he urged.

"If the Prince continues to game with you and is as reprobate as my father, is it not conceivable you could win so much from him you are like to become the next king of England?"

Amanda's fear of treading on toes, particularly those belonging to Lord Glendarvon, proved groundless. All those years of instructing young ladies in the steps of the gavotte, country dance and the cotillion had served to perfect her own mastery of the dances.

The circumstances of her come-out served to make her the object of very great interest. Many of the guests present at the ball recalled the outrageous Sir Nigel Westwood, so when she was partnered by the marquis and stepped out to begin the dancing it was beneath the scrutiny of scores of curious eyes. For once Rose Devine's were not among them. Amanda was glad to see that her cousin was being partnered by Sir Hedley and the girl looked, for once, happy.

After a little initial uncertainty Amanda found the marquis to be an excellent partner. He was as sure-footed as she and after a while she found she enjoyed dancing with him.

When the dance was over he said, looking down at his highly-polished shoes, "Well done, Miss Westwood, not a scuff to be perceived."

She couldn't help but laugh. "What a relief that is to me, my lord. Now I am able to go on and enjoy the remainder of the evening with an untroubled mind."

He led her to the side of the floor. "By all means do." He looked deep into her eyes, which was disconcerting. "I would not want for anything to be the cause of discomfiture to you." In almost every circumstance he was just that and it was a great relief to her when he looked away again, saying, "Ah, here comes Sir Hedley Flint to claim you for the cotillion. No doubt that will please you. I shall go to the card room to relieve a few gentlemen of their purses."

She had drunk deeply of the champagne which was freely available and feeling both light headed and light hearted she chided, responding for once to his teasing, "That is a shabby thing for a host to do."

"On the contrary, Miss Westwood, they drink freely of my champagne, so it is only just that I have some recompense."

"Mayhap they will continue to drink your champagne and then take your purse too."

He nodded in thoughtful agreement. "There is a possibility of that, I own, but only just."

"Ah, Miss Westwood, my set I believe," Sir Hedley greeted her just as the marquis took his leave.

Amanda watched him disappear into the throng around the dance floor and then allowed Sir Hedley to lead her to where the next set was being made up. Despite declaring his intention to retire to the card room, a few moments later the marquis could be seen partnering Rose Devine for the next set. They were not close enough for her to overhear what they were saying to one another, but Amanda could see clearly enough that Rose looked excited, perhaps rather more so than when Sir Hedley partnered her for the previous dance.

In a deliberate manner Amanda turned her back on them both and addressed herself to Sir Hedley. "I was glad to see you partnering my cousin."

"I am not much gratified about that. I had hoped to provoke a little envy in you."

"I could not be so shabby, sir. My cousin harbours a definite fondness for you."

"That is a pity, for she is a fetching chit, but I am bound to confess I am totally bewitched by you, Miss Westwood."

Amanda laughed coquettishly, half turning to note that both her cousin and the marquis were looking at her at that moment. "You are so extravagant in your praise, sir, it is like to turn my head."

"I am genuine in my affection, ma'am, whereas there are many who are not."

To Amanda's relief the music started up and they began to dance, precluding such intense conversation. At intervals they faced the marquis and Rose in the set and invariably Rose glared at her cousin and smiled at Sir Hedley who acknowledged her with only the barest of nods. Amanda could not help but pity the girl. She knew full well if she had lost her heart she would find it unbearable seeing her beloved with another.

After the dance had ended Sir Hedley escorted her back to the side of the floor although he exhibited no anxiety to leave her side. "The gavotte is with Cedric," she explained, in an attempt to keep the conversation in a light vein. "How unfashionable it is to dance with one's brother."

"I am relieved it is he," Sir Hedley responded, "rather than some lovelorn buck eager to steal your heart, although there will be any number of them this evening. Allow me the honour of taking you into supper."

"I should like that very well indeed, Sir Hedley. Ah, here comes my brother now."

Sir Cedric came from the direction of one of the card rooms and Amanda was not unaware of that fact, but she forebore to take him to task on this occasion.

Seeing his friend approaching Sir Hedley still did not relinquish his grip on her arm. "Miss Westwood, there are many gentlemen who will admire you for your grace and beauty, but do, I beg of you, always recall, it is I who has a genuine fondness for you."

Startled by his earnestness Amanda replied,

"It is kind of you to say so, sir, but you have never left me in any doubt of it."

"I do not say it for the sake of kindness, but to let you know my feelings. Moreover, I believe I dare say you are not entirely indifferent to me."

"Sir Hedley, it is far too . . ."

"In the time to come, be assured I will not be found far from your side wherever you may be, Miss Westwood. That is the only place I can be truly happy, when I am close to you."

As she danced with her brother Amanda wondered if she had received a preliminary offer of marriage. If so, it did her self-esteem no harm whatsoever. After the gavotte was ended Sir Cedric took her to meet an acquaintance of his.

"Captain Peregrine Little of the Seventh Dragoons. Perry meet my sister in whose honour tonight's diversion is being held. You have been in a fidge to make her acquaintance all evening."

The soldier, who was handsomely attired in dress uniform, bowed low over her hand. "Delighted, Miss Westwood."

"Perry has just returned from the Peninsula," Sir Cedric explained.

"How do we do there, sir?" she asked.

"Well enough now, Miss Westwood, I am delighted to report. Boney is on the run at last and we shall settle the score fairly soon, I believe."

"That is good news indeed. My aunt will be delighted, for a lack of officers at home plays old Harry with her social plans. Tell me, Captain Little, what brings you back at such a vital juncture?"

"A cracked head which I must hasten to say is completely healed."

Amanda looked shocked. "You were wounded. How dreadful that must have been for you."

Sir Cedric laughed. "Do not allow him to gammon you, Manda. Perry fell off his horse playing the fool with his cronies."

When she stopped laughing she said, "We must not be so unfeeling, for the consequences of such an accident could have been as bad as an encounter with a Frenchie."

"There you are, Westwood!" Captain Little cried. "Your sister has a kindly thought for me even if you do not."

"I thought of you yesterday when I looked to see you at Southwark. John Gulley was fighting Cribb. Excellent mill, I tell you, even if I did wager on the wrong man. You should have seen Cribb give Gulley one in the breadbasket, Little."

"Couldn't make it, Westwood. A great pity I confess but I was engaged to take Lady Honoria Mynton riding in the Park."

"Cedric, I am amazed to hear you admit to gaming again," Amanda told him, her voice full of reproach.

"Not to do so would have been more than I could stand. It was an exceeding good mill."

"Do excuse me, Captain Little," she asked and began to walk away in disgust and disappointment.

Sir Cedric followed. "Don't get into a miff

over this, Manda. It gets me on the raws when you ride grub with me over such a trifle."

"I do not regard persistent gaming as a trifle, Cedric, and you need not trouble trying to grease my boots. I cannot like you gaming, but I do not suppose I can stop you if you are set upon it."

"You may be relieved to know my gaming is curtailed for the present." He looked abashed. "M'pockets are to let, truth to tell. I'm all dished up for the rest of this quarter."

Amanda gave him an exasperated look as he shrugged his shoulders. "Do you truly imagine that is to my relief? If you do you must be a chuckle-head. What is to become of you, Cedric?"

"I'm past praying for, Manda," he admitted but he looked not at all repentant.

Her face relaxed into a smile. "You really deserve to fry in your own grease, but come to see me on the morrow—not too early, mind you. I have some money put by and I dare say it will tide you over until your next allowance is due."

His face took on a look of sheer delight as he hugged her close to him. "Dearest Manda, you are the best sister any fellow could have."

"Recall I have but little, Cedric, so you cannot rely upon me to stump the blunt every time your pockets are to let."

"No, no, it will never happen again, I vow."

Amanda cast him a disbelieving look just as Lady Glendarvon approached, saying, "Miss Westwood, I have someone with me whom you would wish to meet." When Amanda gave her attention to the marchioness's companion she saw he was a very handsome man, as dark as the marquis and as menacing when he was in one of his takings. "I know you are in a fidge to meet Lord Byron and he has condescended to say a few words to you."

Amanda gasped. "Lord Byron, this is indeed the greatest pleasure for me."

The poet nodded curtly in acknowledgement of the introduction and Lady Glendarvon said, "I shall leave you to have a coze."

As she moved away Amanda was intrigued by Lord Byron's appearance. Initially she had thought him to be a little like the marquis, but whereas Lord Glendarvon was always immaculately dressed, the poet appeared to be deliberately unkempt.

"No doubt I shall not be unique in expressing my admiration of your work," Amanda ventured as he scowled around the room.

"It is always gratifying for an artist to be appreciated, Miss Westwood, but I often wonder if I am admired because I am talented, or because I have become all the crack."

Amanda looked shocked. "Oh, I am persuaded your genius is the reason for your becoming fashionable. For myself I can only say I read, no devour, everything you publish."

Out of the corner of her eyes she espied Lord Glendarvon, having returned to the ballroom. Recalling what he had earlier said about Lord Byron she considered it would be the greatest coup if she could contrive for him to dance with her.

"I am to stand up with the Duke of Rokesby

for the country dance," she confided. "Tell me, my lord, shall you be dancing this evening?"

The icy look he gave her would have done justice to the marquis. It was in itself a set-down. "No, Miss Westwood, I do not dance," he said to her dismay and then he walked away.

As he did so one hand flew to her lips, for it was immediately apparent that the poet had a lame foot. He limped quite considerably and could not possibly dance with any grace whatsoever.

"Miss Westwood?"

She tore her horrified gaze away from the poet to see her next partner, the Duke of Rokesby, looking at her curiously. Involuntarily her eyes filled with tears. "Your Grace, I have just committed the most dreadful blunder."

"You, my dear? I cannot conceive how that may be." When she explained the duke merely laughed. "That man is so full of pain I imagine what you said caused him little more," he answered her as he led her onto the dance floor where the sets were being made up for a country dance.

"The evening appears to me to be a resounding success," commented the duke as they took their places.

Amanda's cheeks remained flushed. "Lady Glendarvon has an amazing knack of being successful at all she does."

"You must not minimise your own part in the triumph of the evening, Miss Westwood. Everyone considers your début an exceptional success."

"You are very kind to say so, your Grace, but I owe a good deal to her ladyship."

"As one who is exceeding fond of her, it pleases me to see your gratitude towards her."

"It is evident you are fond of her, your Grace, and she always speaks kindly of you."

"This is even more welcome news. It is no secret that I harbour the greatest fondness for Lady Glendarvon and would marry her if she would have me."

Amanda was not surprised to hear the admission, but she was curious about the relationship. "Mayhap you should ask her, if I may be so bold as to suggest it."

The duke laughed. "Oh, I have asked—even begged—her to condescend to become my wife."

"I cannot begin to conceive why she does not accept with alacrity, your Grace."

"You may be sure I do not lose heart for the future. My affection for her is no fleeting thing."

"It warms my heart to hear you say so," Amanda responded. "Lady Glendarvon, for all her urbanity, is a slightly lonely person, I fear."

"I am persuaded, Miss Westwood, we are in agreement over that. The problem as I perceive it . . . is Lord Glendarvon."

Recalling her aunt's earlier aspersions about their relationship Amanda was startled. "Your Grace, I cannot conceive what you may mean by that."

"That does not surprise me. It is not at all apparent to those not intimate with the couple. Her ladyship has what I believe to be a misguided sense of loyalty to her stepson. She has vowed to remain at his side, to act as his hostess until Lord Glendarvon is himself wed."

At the explanation Amanda let out a long breath so great was her relief.

"That is so like her," she murmured.

"For several years, when she was newly married to his late father, she was obliged to fight for Glendarvon's trust. Once she had won it he came into the title. He was a very young man with a definite bent towards rakishness and Lady Glendarvon felt it incumbent upon her to remain at his side. Those of us who know her should not be surprised at her generosity of spirit, but I would be less than human if I did not pray that Lord Glendarvon will soon find a female to his taste and relieve Lady Glendarvon of what she perceives to be her duty."

Amanda's mind digested this startling information as they began to dance, the lady in question laughing with her current partner, the Prince Regent. After the dance ended and supper was about to be served Amanda heard her aunt say to another lady, "It may well be that Lady Glendarvon is about to oust Lady Hertford and become the Prince's new doxy. Lady Hertford is looking exceeding vexed this evening."

"It would be a role to which she is admirably suited," the other lady responded.

Lady Devine chuckled. "None more so, Adeline."

Amanda had been passing by and turned on her heel to face her aunt who looked startled.

"Aunt Ambrosia, have a heed for whom you insult. Lady Glendarvon is your hostess."

"My dear, I am aware Lady Glendarvon has been a boon to your overweening ambitions, but you must not be blind to her faults, if indeed it is a fault. Prinny is not a prize to be scorned, especially for one of her origins."

Lady Devine looked well pleased with herself but Amanda could only give her a look of disgust. "Lady Glendarvon would be a lady even without her title, which is more than can be said for many of those born to rank."

When Sir Hedley sought her out to take her into supper he observed, "Miss Westwood, you look as mad as a weaver. What can have put you out of countenance on such a splendid evening as this?"

"Nothing of any consequence," she assured him with a smile. "I am famished, however, and Lady Glendarvon has promised that the supper will be exceptional this evening."

"The company certainly will."

Champagne spouted from a fountain and Sir Hedley held out two glasses which swiftly filled with the foaming liquid. As Amanda watched him she laughed. "Sir Hedley, do not, I beg you, give me any more to drink. I believe that I have had sufficient for one evening."

"Drink another with me," he insisted, handing her the glass. "I would wish to make a toast to you. To your future, Miss Westwood, and the hope that we spend it together."

To cover her confusion Amanda said, "La! 'Tis amazing how the champagne continues to flow even when we are at war with the very country which produced it."

"My dear Miss Westwood, is that not why we are fighting the Corsican upstart? If our supplies of claret and champagne cease to flow into our cellars I declare we may as well surrender to that monster with no further delay."

Amanda laughed uneasily, for she felt that the war was not a subject on which they should jest. "I doubt if Wellington and his army would agree with your reasoning, Sir Hedley, but let us hope hostilities will soon cease and all our gallant fighting men are home safe once again."

"Hear, hear!" he agreed, sipping at his champagne a mite too greedily for her liking. "Let us drink a toast to that also."

"Sir Hedley!" she protested. "You will have me foxed."

"Best way to end the evening, you know, ma'am. Perry Little tells me it will all be soon over, never you fear."

"That will be a great relief to us all."

"Miss Westwood, allow me to congratulate you on such a charming début."

Amanda looked round at the speaker to find herself face to face with one of her aunt's cronies, a Mrs. Bosomworth, a lady of great consequence and large wealth. The praise bestowed upon her by one of her aunt's friends caused her cheeks to redden, or perhaps it was the champagne after all. At this point in the evening she could not be quite sure.

"I thank you so kindly, ma'am," Amanda responded with a curtsey. "I do hope you are enjoying the evening yourself."

"How could I not? Lady Glendarvon is always the most welcoming of hostesses. Your very great success this evening must please her very much indeed."

"I am sure it does." She glanced briefly at Sir Hedley who continued to help himself to champagne and then back to Mrs. Bosomworth. "It has been so good of her to take me up."

"Oh yes, I dare say. She has bided her time well, I must own. For so long now she has sought a way of inflicting retribution upon Lady Devine, it seems in you, Miss Westwood, she considers she has at last a weapon of considerable power."

Amanda's ready smile faded. "Mrs. Bosomworth, I regret I do not know what you are insinuating."

The woman smiled with satisfaction. "It is of no real matter, my dear, I assure you. Let us just continue to enjoy ourselves as before and avail ourselves of all the diversions Lady Glendarvon condescends to offer this evening."

So saying she swept away, greeting another acquaintance immediately so that Amanda could not question her further, but her head whirled in an attempt to discover what the woman might have meant by those enigmatic words. She looked around the room which was extremely crowded, unable to see Lady Glendarvon anywhere. Even the Duke of Rokesby was in conversation with another lady.

"Take another glass, Miss Westwood," Sir Hedley invited, "or shall we avail ourselves of the delicacies on the supper table? It is for you to say. I am entirely at your command."

She managed a smile. "No, I thank you, Sir Hedley, but would you excuse me for just a short while? I needs must find Lady Glendarvon on a matter of urgency."

Before the bewildered young man could reply she had hurried away from him seeking out the marchioness as she went. In such a crush of people it was not an easy task. The ballroom was sparsely peopled at that moment so she hurried through the card room, not heeding that Cedric was seated at one of the tables even though he called out a greeting to her. As she searched for Lady Glendarvon, Amanda's need to find her became even more acute. There was something quite significant in what Mrs. Bosomworth had imparted and she was determined to discover what it could be with no further delay.

The marquis was playing faro in one of the rooms and he looked up with interest as she passed by, enquiring quietly of several people the whereabouts of Lady Glendarvon. When she was nowhere to be found in the main rooms, Amanda started down the stairs where she was approached by several of the guests, eager to compliment her. It was all she could do to restrain her impatience as she politely responded to their praise.

Louisa Bell gripped Amanda's hands tightly in her own. "This is the most wonderful diversion," she enthused. "So many of the young men to whom I have spoken are entranced by you, my dear. Do tell, has anyone as yet come up to scratch?"

"It is a trifle too soon for that," Amanda replied and excused herself to continue down the stairs. In the downstairs hall some of the guests were slipping out into the garden, either to take the air or for an assignation. Others were enjoying the relative quiet to be had there.

Amanda had just reached the bottom of the stairs and was wondering where to go next when she heard her name being called. Biting back a gasp of exasperation she turned on her heel to see the marquis standing at the top of the staircase. When she turned to face him he began to walk down the stairs towards her.

"Miss Westwood, you appear to be in something of a pucker. Do tell me what has put you in such a taking."

"Oh no," she quickly assured him, "you are mistaken, my lord."

He gazed into her eyes in that way she found so disturbing. "I think not, my dear."

Amanda looked away in confusion. "It is a trifling matter, of no consequence, I assure you."

"Then why do you seek out Lady Glendarvon with such urgency?"

Several people present in the hall glanced at them curiously. Amanda had come to learn that Lord Glendarvon's activities, however trifling, were of the greatest interest to many of those acquainted with him. She understood that he was considered to be a great matrimonial prize and during recent years many mothers of current débutantes cultivated him quite ruthlessly. Any female, in consequence, with whom he was seen to converse, was the subject of great speculation.

"Well, do you tell me what teases you, or am I obliged to press you further? I do mean to know."

The note of resolution in his voice left her in no doubt about that, something which made her sigh with resignation. "I merely wished to ask Lady Glendarvon for an explanation of something Mrs. Bosomworth said to me a time ago. In all probability it is like she will not know, for it was exceeding enigmatic."

"Mrs. Bosomworth," he repeated thoughtfully, and then, taking her arm, he led her towards an alcove where he drew her down onto a seat. "That lady is renowned for two things. One is the vastness of her husband's slave plantations in the Indies, and the other her waspish tongue. I rather imagine the latter is the source of your megrims."

Still Amanda refused to look at him. "Mrs. Bosomworth implied that I was, in some manner, an instrument of retribution Lady Glendarvon was using against my aunt."

For a long moment he did not say anything and then he drew a deep sigh. "So that is it."

"Is it?" she asked, suddenly insistent. "I do wish someone would be good enough to clarify the matter for me. I have no notion what she may mean."

"Allow me to explain in Lady Glendarvon's absence, Miss Westwood." She knew he was looking at her and she still deliberately averted her gaze from his. "When Lady Glendarvon married my father, there was an influential cabal of ladies in this town who took exception to someone as high born as the Marquis of Glendarvon marrying so far beneath him." As he spoke the restrained anger in his voice was very evident. "They were set upon barring her from every fashionable assembly. Lady Devine and Mrs. Bosomworth were foremost among those ladies, as you might already have guessed. Most fortunately Lady Glendarvon was taken up by those who were even more influential, so her entry into Society was assured."

By the time he had finished his explanation Amanda was shaking with emotion. "How foolish of me to believe I was taken up with the best of intentions for my own sake."

"You were, oh be assured that you were," the marquis answered with surprising passion. "You must not on any account think ill of Lady Glendarvon. She is not so smallminded to use you against Lady Devine. Only Mrs. Bosomworth would think that. After all it was a very long time ago."

"So was the ruination of my father. No doubt you derived a good deal of satisfaction from discomforting his sister!"

"Yes, I did, foolish youth that I was. I regret it now and even then I was determined that his children would not suffer the foolishness of their elders."

"Do not seek to gammon me, my lord. I am not such a green girl. I now know that all you and Lady Glendarvon have done for me is not for my sake, but just to even an old score. You may rest happy to know you have succeeded very well. My aunt could not be more unhappy at my social success."

"You are foolish if you believe that," he said quietly. "You have only to look at yourself in any mirror to know that Lady Glendarvon has done you the greatest kindness. You are the envy of every female here tonight, the object of every gentleman's affection. Everyone is eager to grease your boots. Is that so great a burden to bear?"

Tears began to squeeze from beneath her lids even though she fought valiantly to stop them. "You are hateful," she whispered.

"I have always been sensible of the strength of your dislike, Miss Westwood. You seem to believe I was set upon this earth solely to become a vexation to you. I cannot do anything to change your mind on that score, nor do I intend to try, but do not, I beg of you, think ill of Lady Glendarvon. What she has done for you is out of kindness and compassion and nothing more. If, in the meantime, she can derive a small measure of satisfaction from the situation who can blame her? She is not a saint. Few of us are and we can all make mistakes. If you think you cannot you are a rare creature indeed." The tears continued to slide down her cheeks. After a moment the marquis ordered in a much more strident tone, "Look at me, Miss Westwood." When she did not he went on, "I insist that you do." At last she did raise her eyes to meet his. "I want you to as-

186

sure me you will not be out of humour with Lady Glendarvon over this trifle. You must believe me when I tell you she is not using you and never has. Mrs. Bosomworth's notion was to cause pain and dissension, which she has in full measure. Now, do you believe me?"

Slowly Amanda nodded her head and then she whispered, "Yes, I truly could not believe Lady Glendarvon guilty of any form of treachery. In my heart I knew it could not be so and that is why I sought her out immediately, for I was certain she would explain it to me."

He smiled then and she noted it was a very nice smile, seen all too rarely. At that moment she wondered why she had once thought his mouth was cruel. She was even further surprised when he brought out a lace-edged handkerchief and began to dab at her cheeks.

"You cannot possibly return to the ballroom looking hag-ridden, Miss Westwood. What would the tattle-baskets make of that, I wonder?"

All at once Amanda was aware of his closeness and she was suddenly desperate to move further away from him, but could not do so without inviting his curiosity. Indeed she could not understand it herself.

"There," he said, after what seemed to be a long time dabbing at her tears. "You may keep the handkerchief if you wish."

When he drew away from her she was overwhelmingly relieved and quickly said, "No, I thank you. I have one in my reticule."

As he put away his handkerchief once again he stood up, proffering his arm. "Do you feel equal to returning to the dancing?" She smiled hesitantly and he suggested, "Let us go back upstairs and allow me to stand up with you, Miss Westwood. Let Mrs. Bosomworth and her cronies be confounded by your radiance."

"I would be honoured to stand up with you, my lord," she answered breathlessly, and for once she meant it.

For the first time she looked forward to having him as a partner, knowing all the while she would be watched enviously by all the other débutantes present.

"No, no," he assured her as they walked towards the stairs, "the honour is surely all mine. You are a great success and from now onwards you will surely be the Toast of the Town!"

TWELVE

It was not until dawn was well advanced that
Amanda got to her bed that night. She had
watched the servants lowering the chandeliers
to snuff the candles which were burning low
in their sockets. At that point she had still not
wanted the evening to end so great was her
enjoyment after that brief upset. Besides, she
was beginning to learn that in the *beau monde*
there was a deal of good will but there was
certainly also a good amount of malice. New-
comers were not always welcome even though
that could not truly be said for the Westwood
family, for it was an old name, but fortunately
as the marquis had predicted she had become
popular and that in itself bred satisfaction
among others.

Since the ball countless young men called in
at Park Lane in the hope of being granted a
few minutes of her time. Others left cards,
flowers or marchpane in the hope of finding
favour in her eyes. One of the most insistent
remained Sir Hedley Flint who could always
be relied upon to amuse her.

Much to Amanda's surprise and dismay *The Terrors of Lucifer* became *the* book to be read in the *beau monde*. On the very morning after the ball Lady Glendarvon sent Nel to the circulating library to secure a copy and after reading it declared herself terrified by the tale. Lucy wrote frequently bemoaning the fact that her friend was determined to remain anonymous as she longed to see her receiving public acclaim. Amanda wrote back to tell Lucy of her many activities, of balls and routs, of visits to the opera and musical evenings where she was glad of her own musical ability, for she was invariably called upon to play and sing.

The regular ride in Hyde Park at the fashionable hour was always a pleasure, for so many riders and drivers insisted upon stopping and paying Amanda extravagant compliments. She could not help but be flattered and enjoy it.

"It could not be better," Lady Glendarvon declared one day as they drove out of the park. "You now have a veritable army of admirers, my dear. Do I dare to hope there is one who is special to your heart?"

It was a valid enough question but it did cause Amanda's cheeks to go red when she was obliged to think on the matter. "None of them," she answered truthfully after a moment's consideration. "In any event it is too early for such decisions to be made."

"I do grant you that the Season is not yet old, but Maud Brissom is already betrothed a week after her come-out. Lady Diana Denton is about to announce hers, and I am persuaded neither of them have possessed the number of suitors you have acquired."

Amanda laughed uneasily. "Mayhap it is easier when there are less of them. The choice certainly becomes less complicated."

Lady Glendarvon chuckled and then looked more serious. "I had noted a particular partiality to Sir Hedley Flint. . . ."

Amanda scarcely knew how to answer and before she could the marchioness went on, "I should not be surprised if he comes up to scratch before too long."

For some days now Amanda had also suspected this might be so and she was concerned for she did not love Sir Hedley or any of the others who solicited her affection. Whenever she tried to imagine herself betrothed to Sir Hedley Flint she could only compare him unfavourably with Lord Glendarvon and that was something which alarmed her to a great degree.

"I cannot at this moment say how I would react, my lady," she answered at last. "It is like I should not accept, even though I do find him exceptionally congenial."

"That is a relief, I own. Neither Lord Glendarvon nor myself particularly favour Sir Hedley as a suitor for you. He has a history of pursuing heiresses and as he is so frequently in dun territory his suit is not always welcomed. However, he is most personable, I own, and it is only a matter of time before he is successful with some young lady of means."

Immediately Amanda became irritated. "I

had no notion I was obliged to please Lord Glendarvon in this matter."

The marchioness laughed, not at all put out. "Indeed you are not, my dear, but he is, as I am, concerned for your well-being and future happiness. However, we both wish you to follow your heart." When Amanda made no reply Lady Glendarvon went on in a more serious tone of voice, "You have been in such high snuff of late, seeing you out of humour like this is disturbing to me. Are you quite certain you do not wear the willow for one of those young gentlemen? In all truth, my dear, you display symptoms of being in love."

Once again Amanda laughed uncomfortably. "Faddle, Lady Glendarvon. It is not so, I assure you."

The marchioness drew a deep sigh. "Then I fear you might after all be bearing malice towards me for what Maria Bosomworth told you."

At that moment Amanda had been peering out of the window of the carriage but now she turned to look at the marchioness in alarm, for this was the first time the matter had been mentioned between them. In fact, Amanda hoped and believed Lady Glendarvon remained ignorant of her encounter with Mrs. Bosomworth on the night of the ball.

"So Lord Glendarvon told you of our conversation. I can only regret that, my lady."

"It was not a betrayal of your confidence, I assure you, but he did feel it incumbent upon him to apprise me of the mischief-making which might be afoot. Dear Amanda, I do trust you will not think that my sole reason for giving you a Season was to confound your aunt."

Feeling guilty because it had been her immediate conclusion Amanda hastened to explain, "After I was told the truth of the matter I did assure Lord Glendarvon that I could not believe you to be so devious."

"That is a great relief to me," the marchioness said with feeling so Amanda could not doubt it was so. "I should hate for you to set your face against me."

"That could never be, my lady, and certainly not on the word of one of Lady Devine's cronies."

"Now that is said, I am bound to admit to a feeling of satisfaction at your aunt's discomfiture in this matter, so mayhap my motives are not so altruistic."

"Your feelings are entirely understandable."

"I had considered the matter forgotten. It all happened a long time ago and although it was some time before my stepson would take to me at the outset I have never harboured a grudge against *him*." She laughed and then all at once became serious again. "When I called that day at the Devine's house and witnessed Lady Devine's ill-use of you I could not help but recall that time when I felt so strange and uncertain, and Lady Devine was instrumental in making it so much more difficult for me." She looked at Amanda and smiled again. "It is of no matter now. I have all the influence necessary in this Town and Lady Devine can do nothing to spoil it."

Amanda took a deep breath before saying, "You have that as well as the love of a good man, my lady."

The marchioness looked at her in some surprise. "It is your matrimonial arrangements which interest me."

"I must beg your pardon for being so bold, my lady, but you are surely aware of his Grace's feelings towards you. He harbours a great fondness for you."

Lady Glendarvon cast her a mocking look and Amanda could only be glad she was not angry at her presumption. "Has he now appointed a green girl to plead his case for him?"

"Indeed not," Amanda answered, bridling at the suggestion. "His Grace would not be so foolish, but it is not like you to be so cruel to one who cares so deeply."

Lady Glendarvon patted Amanda's hand reassuringly. "You need not concern yourself on Rokesby's behalf. Let me assure you the matter will be decided very soon."

"Favourably I trust, my lady."

The marchioness cast her a maddening smile. "I believe you can assume that to be so, and not just for Rokesby and myself, I fancy."

All at once Amanda became alert. "That means . . . you must believe . . ."

The marchioness looked wide-eyed and innocent. "Yes, my dear?"

Quickly Amanda looked away. "It is nothing of import, my lady."

When the carriage came to a halt at the entrance to Lord Elgin's Park Lane mansion

Amanda felt even more confused. "Why are we stopping here?"

"Have you not heard? Lord Elgin has returned from Europe with a wondrous collection of art including marble friezes from the Parthenon in Athens and he has been good enough to invite everyone who wishes to see them. I am persuaded the exhibition will be fascinating and you would not wish to miss the event."

At any other time Amanda would have enthusiastically agreed, but just at that moment her head was full of what the marchioness had told her. In all truth she was not certain exactly what she had been told. Did Lady Glendarvon expect the marquis to announce his own betrothal in the near future? If so, to whom? Amanda had never witnessed his partiality to any female who could be considered remotely eligible.

Many other fashionables were making their visit to Lord Elgin's manisons, one being the Duke of Rokesby and there was no mistaking his pleasure in seeing the marchioness as they entered the hall.

"What good fortune this is," he greeted them.

"Is it not?" agreed Lady Glendarvon who cast Amanda a wry glance.

"Miss Devine's ball was a great success," the duke told Amanda as they walked up the stairs to the salon where the treasures were being displayed.

"You may be sure, your Grace, that is of the greatest relief to me."

"I think it must be pointed out that Miss Westwood is in some measure responsible for its success," mused Lady Glendarvon. "as it was she who made many of the arrangements before she left Devine House."

"Then it is all credit to you, ma'am," the duke responded.

Amanda couldn't help but laugh. "It's not likely I shall receive credit from any other source on that score, but had it been a failure no doubt I should have been blamed, and in a very loud manner too."

When they reached the top of the stairs none other than Lady Devine and her daughter were seen about to depart. Their eyes became cold when they espied Amanda, but because of the many mutual acquaintances milling around they were obliged to acknowledge her. After the preliminary niceties were over Lady Glendarvon and the duke wandered away, leaving Amanda to face them alone.

"I did so enjoy your ball, Rose," Amanda enthused, anxious to breach the rift in their relationship. "Everyone acknowledges it was a great success. His Grace was only just saying so to me a moment ago."

"We did note you were enjoying yourself," her aunt pointed out, exhibiting no pleasure in the face. "Lord Glendarvon's conscience must be a burdensome thing for him to bear."

Amanda's smile faded somewhat at the mention of someone who plagued her thoughts in the most troublesome way of late. "I do not understand what you might mean by that, Aunt."

"I noted that he danced with you on several occasions. Evidently he feels it necessary for his patronage to be seen by all if you are to continue to have a successful Season."

"But he also danced with me, Mama," Rose pointed out, looking petulant.

"Well, it was *your* come-out ball," her mother replied, "and Lord Glendarvon certainly had no obligation towards you. When he stood up with you it could only have been a matter of pleasure, my dear."

The thought that duty alone had prompted his attentiveness caused Amanda's eyes to cloud. Since her own ball their relationship had become somewhat easier, and she could only be glad of that.

Rose's manner positively bristled with malice. "The *on-dits* have it that Sir Hedley Flint is about to make an offer for you. The wagers in the book at White's expect it within the sen'night."

Again Amanda became confused. "I cannot say. . . ."

"He will be obliged to ask Papa's permission," Rose pointed out.

"Yes, I presume any gentleman who comes up to scratch will be obliged to do that," Amanda replied recovering some of her composure. "and I do not doubt Sir Giles will accept on my behalf."

She swept past them as Rose could be heard to wail, "Not Sir Hedley, Mama. I cannot bear it."

"Tush!" her mother replied unsympathetically. "There are better men for you, my dear.

197

On the other hand your cousin is deserving of that scapegrace."

Amanda bit her lip, wondering why she could not derive any satisfaction from this situation, but the fact remained she suddenly felt as miserable as her cousin appeared to be, and reason told her it should not be so.

"Miss Westwood, come see what I have purchased this afternoon!" She looked up to see Lady Cottesley bearing down on her. "*The Terrors of Lucifer.* I shall cry off this evening's diversion at Vauxhall so I may read it for myself and perceive what all the fuss and botheration is about." The reminder of the success of the novel was just the thing to cast Amanda into a deeper despair. "Have you by any chance read it yet, Miss Westwood?" She was bound to admit that she had. "Is it as good as people say of it?" the woman asked eagerly.

"Oh indeed," she answered heavily and the woman hurried off, well-pleased with herself.

Amanda found Lady Glendarvon and the duke listening to a description of the treasures from Lord Elgin himself and they attended him closely while Amanda inspected the broken marble tablets with all the others milling around.

At last she could not help but ask, "Would it not have been better to leave them in their rightful place, my lord?"

The earl was not in the least put out. "That would have deprived a good many people of the pleasure of seeing them, my dear. In any event, the Turks who presently occupy Greece are a barbarous lot with no feeling for art.

They have already destroyed so much I deemed it prudent to rescue these treasures before it is too late."

"What a happy circumstance you did," the marchioness agreed.

Lord Elgin wandered away to greet more of his visitors while Amanda inspected the frescoes more closely. As she did so a voice close by said, "Magnificient, are they not?"

She straightened up to find Lord Byron nearby. Amanda still felt embarrassed after their last encounter but he did not seem to bear her a grudge. His eyes burned with intensity as he stared at the tablets.

"I confess I am much impressed," she replied, looking askance at the poet's appearance which, as on the previous occasion she had seen him, was less than immaculate.

"The sight of these marvels fires my imagination, Miss Westwood. I have it in mind to visit that country."

"It is a very long way, my lord, and the journey is fraught with danger, I fear."

"So much the better. There is so much injustice in the world. It is time the native Greeks got back their own country. Imagine if Boney was to invade England. It is not to be borne, I tell you."

He was summoned away by an acquaintance and as he limped across the room Amanda was once again assailed by remorse for her careless remark on the other evening.

"He always appears to be in high dudgeon," Lady Glendarvon pointed out when she returned to Amanda's side. "It is said he is in search of a wife now that he and Lady Oxford have parted company. Lady Melbourne is determined to try and arrange a match for him, but I fancy that is only because her daughter-in-law, Carol Lamb, has a fancy for him. In all truth, Amanda, I cannot conceive of how he may win anyone's heart when he always appears to be so out of humour."

"There are many who would be glad to be allied to a genius."

"Oh indeed, there are many ladies, both young and old, who throw themselves at his head."

"If you are in a mind to curry favour on my behalf I must tell you he declares his intention of going to Greece."

"How like him that is, and I do not believe for one moment he would make a good match for you, my dear." She raised her quizzing glass and peered at the poet across the room. "I wonder what Brummel would make of him."

"What would he make of Brummel," Amanda countered, much to the marchioness's amusement.

A moment later she turned to Amanda. "My dear, we are engaged to attend Lady Harpenden's soirée this evening. She has contrived to engage Signora Catalini to sing, so I'm persuaded we must return to Glendarvon House to dress with no further delay."

"Where is his Grace?" Amanda asked as they took their leave of Lord Elgin.

"He has departed ahead of us, but have no fear," she added wryly, "we will encounter him once again at Harpenden House this evening."

Abashed by the marchioness's good-natured teasing Amanda began to chatter inconsequentially. "Signora Catalini. How famous! I hear that her singing is as sweet as a nightingale's."

"That is undoubtedly so. However, as on so many occasions the tattle will all be of Emily Godrington and who she may be. The rumours are becoming ridiculous. Some say she is really a man, others that she is a duchess."

"Is it of any consequence?" Amanda asked, injecting a false note of lightness into her voice.

"No, I think not, but I did enjoy the book, I confess, and it would be nice to know exactly who the author is and I cannot conceive how it can be she doesn't wish to be acclaimed."

"Whoever she is we shall be obliged to respect her wishes on that score," Amanda pointed out.

Their conversation died away abruptly when they reached the head of the stairs on their way out, for coming towards them was Lord Glendarvon and accompanying him was the most exquisite creature Amanda had ever seen. A pale heart-shaped face dominated by a pair of huge violet blue eyes was framed by a halo of dark curls, and her curvaceous figure was clad in an elegant velvet gown and ermine tippet. All those who passed them on the stairs paused to stare at her.

Amanda recognised her immediately—Violet Pettigrew. Everyone in the *beau monde* knew of Mrs. Pettigrew, who was no older than Amanda herself. The Town was agog with gossip about the young widow of a city merchant who had been left unimaginably wealthy by her husband's demise and was now dangling after a title. It seemed certain that she would soon be elevated to one, for so many gentlemen of the *ton*, particularly impoverished ones, flocked to her door, but there were also many like the marquis who vied for her favour just for the pleasure of her company. In all truth Amanda could not blame them, for there could be no one else to compare with her for beauty.

"Lady Glendarvon, Miss Westwood, allow me to introduce Mrs. Pettigrew," the marquis said, looking well-pleased with himself for having secured her company in the face of so much aristocratic competition.

As the marchioness acknowledged the introduction Mrs. Pettigrew bobbed a curtsey. "I am in a fidge to see Lord Elgin's treasures," the gorgeous creature enthused. "Are they truly as amazing as everyone says?"

"You will be obliged to decide for yourself," Lady Glendarvon told her, "but I will say they are very well executed considering they are so old."

Mrs Pettigrew looked shocked. "Old? How old?"

"Something more than one thousand years," Lord Glendarvon told her.

"I had no notion they were old at all," she gasped. "From all you have told me I had it in mind Lord Elgin had commissioned them from an artist he encountered when on his travels."

At last Amanda broke her silence. "I am persuaded that if Lord Elgin was of a mind to commission new artifacts he would have made certain they were unbroken ones."

The marquis looked amused but merely said, touching Mrs. Pettigrew's arm lightly, "Come along, my dear, let us go to judge for ourselves."

He bowed to the two ladies and Mrs. Pettigrew executed an elegant curtsey. As they moved away Amanda could hear the beauty say, "I cannot conceive why Lord Elgin would want to convey such old artifacts all the way to England. Everything in my house is new; I insisted upon it."

The marquis's reply could not be heard but as Amanda and Lady Glendarvon moved down the stairs, the marchioness remarked, "Much has been said of her wealth and her beauty, but no one has made mention of her intellect."

"Mayhap that is due entirely to gentlemen not taking note of it."

The marchioness cast her a shrewd look. "The same cannot be said of you, my dear. Your intellect is of the highest order."

"There are times when I wished it otherwise."

As they awaited the Glendarvon carriage, the marchioness mused, "Intellect is often partnered by an excess of sensibility, I fear."

Lady Glendarvon's carriage rumbled towards them and when it stopped a footman handed first the marchioness and then Amanda into it. As she sank back into the squabs for the short journey back to Glendarvon House she acknowledged that Mrs. Pettigrew might well be the reason Lady

Glendarvon was confident she would soon be able to make the Duke of Rokesby happy. Moreover, knowing his stepmother wanted to marry might just be the spur to Lord Glendarvon's own matrimonial announcement. Only a lady of great wealth and beauty could possibly coax him away from his precious bachelor status. Mrs. Pettigrew fitted that description admirably, Amanda was bound to admit, but the realisation for her, at least, was not a happy one.

THIRTEEN

Almacks' Assembly Rooms. The great shrine of exclusiveness was open to Amanda and she could not help but be excited by the prospect of attending one of the assemblies. Entry to the gatherings held there on Wednesday evenings was closely guarded by the high-born patronesses. Exemplary behaviour from those young ladies who aspired to attend was mandatory, although the patronesses themselves who issued vouchers for entry did not necessarily subscribe to the strict moral code. However, every débutant anxiously vied for the right of entry. Amanda, being Lady Glendarvon's protégée had no such anxieties, but on her first visit to the hallowed assembly she could not help but feel no small amount of satisfaction.

It had become a habit for Lady Veronica to watch her get ready for her evenings out. In fact Amanda had come to rely upon the girl to help her choose the correct pieces of jewelry to match each ensemble. It was already apparent that Lady Veronica had inherited her mother's good taste.

"How I wish I was going to Almacks tonight," the child said wistfully as Amanda applied a modicum of rouge to her cheeks with a hare's foot.

"Your come-out will arrive soon enough," she told her, "and then you will have any number of assemblies to attend, not only Almacks."

"But that is the one to which we all aspire. Without a voucher for Almacks a Season is all but ruined."

"You should have no cause for alarm, for *your* entry is assured."

"It will be so wonderful standing up with all those handsome bucks. It must be near impossible to favour only the one."

"No, it is not," Amanda answered, her tone suddenly muted.

Lady Veronica's eyes gleamed with speculation. "Then you have decided upon one of them."

"No, I have not," Amanda answered hurriedly.

"*Are* you in love?" the girl persisted.

Amanda was beginning to feel more than a little uncomfortable. "Indeed not."

"Will you vow to tell me when you are?"

"When it happens, if it does, I will think on it. Do you not think you should return to the nursery, dearest?"

"When you are all gone to Almacks I am going to read *The Terrors of Lucifer*. I have Mama's copy. Have you read it yet, Amanda?"

She turned round on the stool. "Yes, I have, and in my opinion it is not in the least suitable for a girl of your tender years."

The pronouncement only served to make the girl laugh. "I read all the Gothic novels, but I believe this one is particularly frightening. Everyone is talking about it and wondering who Miss Emily Godrington really is."

"You really are past praying for," Amanda told her with a laugh, "and if I remain here chattering with you I am like to be late which would never do for Almacks not to mention your mother and brother who are waiting for me!"

When she came down the stairs she felt both elated and despondent. The elation was easily understood; she was, after all, a great social success in a fickle society, the despondency less so. Amanda decided she must be in a fidge lest it be revealed that she was, in fact, the famous Emily Godrington.

Seeing the marquis, resplendent in evening dress awaiting her in the hall, did nothing to ease her disquiet. Quite to the contrary she found the sight of him added to it. Amanda reasoned that it was fear of his anger if he ever discovered she had used him as a model for the ghastly villain of her tale which caused her such unease while common sense told her that in the unlikely event he even read the book he couldn't possibly recognise himself, so great was the caricature. She was human enough to regret writing it despite the success of the novel. The tattle-baskets were saying that Miss Austen was about to publish another novel in the near future and Amanda could only hope that when it appeared her own would sink into very welcome obscurity.

"You look utterly charming, Cecilia," the marquis greeted his stepmother who received the compliment with her customary graciousness. Then he turned his attention to Amanda who before he even spoke grew rather pink. "No doubt this evening will be another triumph for you, Miss Westwood."

Averting her eyes from his she murmured, "I thank you, my lord."

She could not help but recall his solicitous attitude towards her on the night of her come-out ball. He had displayed a facet of his character she had never seen before, but Amanda couldn't help but wish they could find such accord again.

"It promises to be quite a hurricane tonight," ventured the marchioness as the carriage set off.

"Nonsense," the marquis contradicted. "It will be as dull as ever it is."

Amanda glanced across at Lord Glendarvon who was peering out of the window. Running footmen carrying flaming torches preceded the carriage through the streets to light the coachman's way.

"Did Mrs. Pettigrew enjoy viewing Lord Elgin's treasures, my lord?" she asked, giving in to the small streak of malice she felt towards the young woman.

He turned to give her a bland look. As was usual nothing could be elicited from his manner. "I believe that she did, although she still

208

cannot conceive why his lordship wished to display with so much pride what she described as broken stones."

Lady Glendarvon looked amused but it was Amanda who could not stifle her laughter. A moment later, becoming serious again, she said, "I do beg your pardon, my lord. Mayhap, Mrs. Pettigrew will find this evening's diversion more to her taste."

"I very much doubt that Mrs. Pettigrew will gain entry to Almacks," Lady Glendarvon pointed out, "unless the patronesses have had a great change of policy, which I very much doubt."

"How sad that is when she is all the rage."

"If you feel so strongly on the matter mayhap I shall have words with my dear friend Lady Jersey."

The marquis returned to gaze out of the window as if the matter was of no interest to him. His apparent disinterest seemed meaningful to Amanda.

"It is nothing to me," she assured the marchioness. "No doubt when . . . if Mrs. Pettigrew makes an advantageous marriage she will then be accepted everywhere."

"Oh very true," Lady Glendarvon agreed but the marquis continued to remain aloof from the conversation.

While it was very provoking that she could elicit no response from him on the subject of Mrs. Pettigrew she became positively alarmed when he at last turned to his stepmother and said, "Cecilia, I am concerned for Veronica. When I went to bid her goodnight this evening

209

I found her reading a novel called *The Terrors of Lucifer*. Do you know of it?"

"Indeed I do. Few ladies of the *ton* do not, my dear."

"I'm not certain it is good for her to be addicted to such reading matter."

"Nor I, but she enjoys it so," the marchioness replied.

"I wish she would attend her schoolbooks with such assiduity."

"The novel is all the crack now," the marchioness explained. "*Entre nous* I enjoyed it myself. When I was walking along Picadilly the other day Hatchard's bow window was full of them and the circulating library is constantly out of stock. The most interesting thing is the speculation upon who Miss Emily Godrington really can be. The latest *on-dit* attributes her to being a member of the *ton* but I cannot hold that it is like to be so."

Throughout the conversation between Lord Glendarvon and his stepmother on the subject of her novel Amanda had sunk further into the squabs, affecting not to be interested in the subject. When the marquis addressed her at last she started visibly, for every mention of *The Terrors of Lucifer* was painful to her.

"Have you read this literary wonder, Miss Westwood!"

"Yes, yes indeed," she answered, studiously averting her gaze from his probing look.

"Do you enjoy such fantasies?" he persisted.

"I prefer Miss Austen, I own."

"And do you have any thoughts on who the author may be?"

Before Amanda could think of a suitable reply Lady Glendarvon said, "Tush. Miss Westwood has been in London such a short time. How could she possibly be expected to hazard a guess when all the *ton* are nonplussed by the puzzle. La! Here we are at last. This promises to be an interesting evening."

"If it does it will be the very first time at Almacks," the marquis responded.

They joined the great press of people eager to go in. Amanda had become acquainted with a great many people since coming out into Society and was glad to greet some of them, for doing so diverted her mind from the matters which plagued her.

Sir Hedley Flint immediately claimed her for the Scottish reel. Of late Amanda had found his company rather less diverting than before, owing to the fact he had become a little too intense for her comfort, although she could easily understand his motives. What she would do if one of her many suitors offered marriage she did not dare to think.

"All the other females here tonight must be in high dudgeon, Miss Westwood," Sir Hedley told her. "When you are present they simply cease to exist."

"That is both unkind and untrue," she retorted. "I am given to understand my cousin, Miss Devine, has already received three offers of marriage."

"The gentlemen concerned cannot be of any consequence, ma'am, else the lady would have accepted one of them."

"Mayhap she is simply in love with another."

"Then I most heartily sympathise, for I know full well what it is to suffer the pangs of passion."

"What a tongue-pad you are, Sir Hedley."

To her relief the reel began and conversation was precluded. At the end of the reel she was claimed by Captain Little for the cotillion and then a Mr. Arbuthnot for the country dance. By the time the gentlemen were taking their partners for the new sensation, the waltz, Amanda was breathless and her head in a positive whirl. The opportunity of sitting out this particular dance was very welcome and as she sought out a seat she heard one matron remark:

"Even after Lady Jersey's tacit approval of the dance I still maintain no lady would behave in such an immoral manner."

However Amanda noted that Lady Jersey had taken to the floor together with one or two other ladies of influence.

"Come Miss Westwood," whispered a voice in her ear, "let us show them how it is to be danced."

Startled to see that it was the marquis at her side, Amanda immediately began to back away. "Oh no, I beg of you, I cannot . . ."

It was all very well for Lady Jersey and some of the other matrons of the *ton* to dance the waltz, but for a débutante dependent upon their good will it could be an act of utter folly. Moreover, standing up with Lord Glendarvon would only compound her confusion as he was likely to be in the forefront of those condemning her wanton behaviour had she danced the waltz with anyone else. However, as was usual the marquis was not to be gainsaid and as he led her onto the dance floor, less crowded than before, Amanda caught sight of Lady Glendarvon stepping forward to shake her head in their direction, but it was too late. The music had begun. The marquis grasped her by the waist and drew her close to him. The sweet smell of his eau-de-cologne made her head swim and to be held so close was even more discomforting.

"This is a far more congenial manner of dancing, Miss Westwood," he murmured as he gazed down into her eyes. "Do you not agree?"

She was unable to reply for she was all at once breathless, quite unaware of all the eager eyes watching them. As he swung her round to the strains of the music it seemed they were the only two people on the floor. As the music swept her up she became oblivious to any disapproval she might attract and she began to enjoy herself. She became elated and unaware of many of the hostile stares around her, the whispers being conducted behind open fans.

As the last strains of the waltz died away she heard the familiar voice of her aunt saying to Rose, who stared at Amanda with her usual hostility, "I always suspected Amanda was a flighty baggage. It must be hereditary, for my poor dead brother had a decidedly immoral streak."

Amanda's elation disappeared at that moment, for she was aware that there might be many others who would regard her in a similar way to her aunt, and Lady Devine could be relied upon to perpetuate the myth. Looking up into the smiling eyes of her partner who seemed somewhat reluctant to relinquish his hold on her, she asked imploringly, "Lord Glendarvon, have I committed a blunder?"

"How can you possibly think so? Nothing can spoil your triumph now."

Amanda was not so sure and when she looked around to see Lady Jersey moving purposefully towards them she began to tremble with fear.

"Miss Westwood," Lady Jersey began, "you executed those steps splendidly. How I wish I could dance with such lightness and grace."

Amanda's smile was one of sheer relief. If she had disgraced herself it would have only reflected upon Lady Glendarvon and Amanda would not for anything have wanted that. In any event, in retrospect, it was not unlikely that the marquis would have encouraged her to behave in an improper manner.

"You are very generous, my lady, but I feel obliged to point out your own grace embraces everything you do."

Lady Jersey looked delighted at the compliment. "We must have a coze when time permits but for now do excuse me, Miss Westwood, Lord Glendarvon."

When she had gone the marquis looked at her in amazement. "Is there anyone you cannot charm with a few well-considered words?"

All at once Amanda's flush of happiness melted away. "Indeed there are those who scorn me, but I can do nothing about the matter and I do not intend to allow it to tease me any more."

"Well said, but if you refer to your relatives, Miss Westwood, they are truly not worthy of the consideration. No doubt you have noted their presence here tonight which is due entirely to Lady Glendarvon's benevolence."

"I am aware of that. She is remarkable generous. May I now be excused, my lord?"

She was about to leave his side when he said in a low tone, "Miss Westwood, can you imagine the confusion which would ensue here tonight if I were to announce the presence of the very elusive Miss Emily Godrington?"

Shock rooted Amanda to the spot. At last she asked in a harsh whisper, "What do you mean?"

"So you do not deny that you are she?"

"How did you discover her identity?" Amanda asked, still hoping to forestall him.

" 'Twas remarkable easy," he answered with maddening complacency. "When the excitement over the novel began and I took note of it, the name was somehow familiar to me although at first I could not understand why. Then, after a little thought on the matter, I recalled that one of the Westwood family names happened to be Godrington. Your father for instance was Sir Nigel Anthony Charles Godrington Westwood. Do correct me if I am wrong." Amanda remained silent but her expression was mutinous. When a Mr. Carmichael approached Amanda, no doubt to engage her for a dance, the marquis turned briefly to him and charmingly said, "Carmichael, be so good as to return a little later. Miss Westwood and I are engaged in a coze of some import." Then turning to her again he went on, "Emily is one of your own names, is it not?"

"I cannot deny what you have said, but it is a tenuous connection to say the least."

"Indeed, you are quite correct, but not so tenuous when I am informed by my old friend Mr. Long of the Minerva Press that his new author is a teacher at an academy at Alysford in Gloucestershire, who, for reasons unspecified, wishes to keep her identity a secret." There was nothing she could say and a moment later he added, "Am I to assume by your very silence I am correct?"

"You already knew you were before you even broached the subject," she accused, wondering how she could have ever learned to have trusted such a treacherous man.

"I cannot perceive why you are in such a fidge to remain anonymous, Miss Westwood. There are few who are not loud in their praise of Miss Godrington."

"The novel was never intended to be published. Indeed I never intended that anyone should read it," she said in a low, urgent voice. "My friend at Alysford, Mrs. Brandfoot, sent in the manuscript after I had left for London. It was none of my doing. I knew nothing of the matter until she informed me it was to be published and even then I would have stopped publication except that my chill which I contracted the day you found me in Bond Street delayed my contacting Mr. Long and by the time that I did it was too late to stop it."

"I still cannot conceive why you should want to. Last night I read the terrifying tale myself and was most impressed by its inventiveness, but tell me do if it is entirely a work of your own imagination or have you personally experienced such fiendish treatment?"

It was impossible for her to meet his mocking gaze or answer him with any degree of equanimity, so regardless of her dignity she turned on her heel and rushed from the room.

Her cheeks had flamed to an umbecoming red. He knew! Amanda put two hands to her cheeks in a useless effort to cool them. She couldn't envisage even being able to face him again with any equanimity whatsoever. Her situation had been one of a certain discomfort since coming to London, but all at once it had become intolerable and what was worse she could see no way out of it. She felt as trapped as a butterfly in a cage.

It was Sir Hedley Flint who stopped her flight. "Miss Westwood, what good fortune to find you alone. Allow me the honour of taking you into supper now it is being served."

"Oh, Sir Hedley, I am in such a taking."

"Over a mere dance?" he scoffed. "You were, as always, utterly charming. A year ago perhaps it might well have been damaging to you, but not now. I and many others were entranced by you and could only envy his lordship his partner. Set your mind at rest and let us take some refreshment."

Glad to have such an interpretation put upon

her discomfiture Amanda gladly acquiesced. The relative quiet in the supper room was most welcome although she kept casting anxious glances at the entrance in the event Lord Glendarvon should come in. She was glad for every minute he did not, but she was not so distraught she didn't note that the supper provided was totally unexceptional.

Sir Hedley brought her some of the lemonade and bread and butter which was on offer and although she drank some of the lemonade thankfully she could not touch a morsel of the food.

"Why is my brother not here tonight, Sir Hedley?" she managed to ask at last.

Even as she spoke she wondered if the marquis was at that moment divulging her secret to all those present. Her knowledge of him told her he would keep her secret and use it to taunt her whenever he could. Public discovery would be preferable to that.

"Sir Cedric had another engagement, ma'am."

"Do you know where he is to be found?" When Sir Hedley hesitated to answer she warned, "Do not seek to gammon me on this."

"Miss Westwood," he conceded, "I do know how Sir Cedric's behaviour teases you even though it is not, I assure you, out of the ordinary. I am persuaded, however, that a brother-in-law might well hold more sway with him in such matters than a mere acquaintance." Before a startled Amanda could respond he went on, his voice low with urgency, "You must be aware that I lost my heart to you the very moment we first met. Your uncle is present this evening and I have it in mind to make an offer with no further delay."

Still Amanda could say nothing. The now familiar feeling of bleakness assailed her although now it was clear why she felt so bereft.

"Miss Westwood, this cannot come as a surprise to you, but if you tell me the notion of becoming Lady Flint is repugnant to you I shall heed your wishes and not embarrass you any further, but I do dare to hope it is not so."

As he spoke Amanda suddenly saw a way out of the dilemma. If she were to marry him she would be well out of the marquis's way for good, away from him and Mrs. Pettigrew when she took her place as mistress of Glendarvon House. Amanda knew with great certainty she could not bear to remain under his roof when that came to be, so she may as well marry Sir Hedley Flint and be done with it. She had never expected to marry, much less fall in love, so a marriage to Sir Hedley Flint would be far more than she could have possibly hoped for such a short time ago.

Tears trembled on her lashes. "It would certainly not be repugnant to me, Sir Hedley, if you honoured me with an offer of marriage."

"Then I shall delay no longer and seek out Sir Giles immediately, if you would be kind enough to excuse me, Miss Westwood."

"Yes, by all means," she answered in a dull voice. "Let it be done."

She watched him go, her eyes filling with tears again. Her début had been everything a girl could have wished and she was aware most of her acquaintances expected to see her wed into a position of power and wealth, but it seemed to Amanda if she could not have the man she really loved she may as well marry the one with whom she dealt so well. She didn't doubt that Sir Giles would accept the offer with alacrity. Seeing her married to a relative nonentity such as Sir Hedley Flint would suit them only too well, in addition to removing him from Rose's sight.

For everyone concerned it was the most satisfactory solution, but despite that knowledge Amanda felt more unhappy than she could ever recall. Her despair at the time of her father's ruination did not compare, nor did the passion attached to her hatred of the marquis. That feeling could not compare at all with the overwhelming love she had come to feel for him since.

FOURTEEN

Amanda lost count of the time she remained in the supper room, smiling absently whenever someone greeted her, but when she saw the marquis enter the room and begin to look around she slipped out of the nearby door. In the lobby she sank back against a marble pillar, relishing the feel of its coolness through the thin muslin of her gown. Music filtered out from the ballroom and she was vaguely aware she was engaged for the country dance with Lord Danby, but all she could think about was her own misery and to wonder if Sir Hedley had located her uncle yet.

A footstep nearby made her stand up straight and catch her breath which had been somewhat uneven. Her heart began to flutter more unevenly when she saw the marquis coming towards her, but flight was impossible. There was nowhere to go, save the ballroom, and to do so would have involved passing him.

"Sir Hedley Flint has just informed me he is

about to offer for you," he said, his manner totally inscrutable.

Amanda adjusted her shawl and answered in a less than steady voice, "That is so."

"Am I to understand it is with your knowledge and consent that he does this?"

"Indeed it is. Sir Hedley was most punctilious in ascertaining my feelings on the matter. I would have expected no less from him."

"Amanda." His voice was low and urgent and she stared at his use of her name. "You cannot think to marry Sir Hedley Flint."

She looked at him at last, her eyes blazing into his dark ones. "Why not indeed? He is most affable and devoted to me."

"I do not doubt that for one moment, but he is certainly not worthy of you."

Amanda drew herself up proudly. "Who are you to say who is worthy, my lord?"

"Allow me greater knowledge than you," he replied, "And I am persuaded such a match will not do."

"If I wish to throw my cap over the windmill I will not seek leave from you first, I assure you. I do not tell you to disassociate yourself from Mrs. Pettigrew because she is a chucklehead. No, my lord, you will not dictate to me whom I shall accept or not. In any event you are far too late."

She would have brushed past him then only he caught her by the wrist and drew her back towards him. His inscrutability was no more. The fury was plain to see in his face.

"If you insist upon allying yourself to that

fool you will have one memory to keep by you in the future."

Amanda was afraid and demanded, "Unhand me," as he pulled her ever closer towards him, but then, when his lips claimed hers, she could no longer utter any sound nor did she want to. After that initial protest she didn't even struggle. When he relinquished his grip on her wrist his arms encircled her waist, holding her prisoner to his passion. Amanda had no notion how long they stood clasped in each other's arms for it was no longer a matter of the marquis forcing her into submission. She gladly melted into his embrace, marvelling at the emotion liberated in her by so bruising a kiss.

Even when someone approached, the marquis did not relinquish his hold upon her, only when an angry voice demanded, "Gad sir, what is the meaning of this outrage?" did Amanda step back and was freed at last from his embrace.

Hurrying towards them was Sir Giles and Sir Hedley and they were both red-faced with anger.

"You will meet me over this," Sir Hedley vowed and Amanda cried, "Oh, I pray you do not be so foolish."

"The lady is wise," the marquis said in a warning tone. "Such action may well cost you your life, sir, and to what avail when Miss Westwood has declared her intentions of becoming leg-shackled to you? Be assured the lady was a most unwilling partner and I admit to being brutish with her."

"Then you shall certainly meet me! Sir Giles will be my second. Name yours, Glendarvon, before I declare you a coward!"

"Gentlemen. Gentlemen." Lady Glendarvon came hurrying towards them just as the marquis's eyes narrowed dangerously at Sir Hedley's accusation. "Let us not be hasty."

The marquis relaxed somewhat with the arrival of his stepmother, taking out his snuffbox and savouring a pinch.

Amanda was beyond listening to any more and what is more she was utterly confused. They were quarrelling over her and yet it seemed she was the last person anyone considered. She could bear it no more and hurried away from them all without being seen to go. She rushed out of the building and summoned a hackney carriage instructing the jarvey to drive her back to Glendarvon House. Escape to the house in Park Lane was only a brief respite, she realised, but there was nowhere else for her to go. *The Terrors of Lucifer* had become a great success, but her fee from that alone would not give her an independence.

As confused as she was, on one matter Amanda was thinking clearly enough to know she had been a fool to think she could marry Sir Hedley. Such a short time ago she had been prepared to enter a convivial marriage to a man who merely amused her. Now she knew it would not do, not for her in any event. She wanted to love utterly and be loved in return. Nothing else would now suffice. The marquis had liberated in her a passion she had never known existed. Even now her lips tingled from his kiss and she trembled at the memory of what it had done to her.

Large tears began to furrow down her cheeks at the memory of being held close to him and the strength of his embrace, but she had to remember that his feelings did not match her own. She came to realise, on learning he would be obliged to bestow her huge dowry on Sir Hedley Flint, he had reverted to his naturally reprobate self. All that charm and pleasantness was an act worthy of John Philip Kemble. Pressed by Lady Glendarvon he had offered a large portion on her behalf, but Amanda now saw he did not intend to pay it, not to Sir Hedley Flint, not to any man. He would thwart all possible betrothals with any means in his power. Tonight was a good enough example of that. The portion would, of course, always remain attached to her name, but he would ensure it was never handed over. Amanda saw her fate quite clearly then; she would die an old maid, bitter and lonely. How she hated him and loved him at one and the same time, and what pity she felt for her own miserable situation.

Back at Almacks no one had as yet noticed her absence. Sir Giles and Sir Hedley Flint stared angrily at the marquis who continued to affect an indifferent air.

"Make up your mind, Flint," he said at last. "Do you or do you not wish to call me out? I would like to end this rather trying evening."

"You show no remorse for ravishing my

bride-to-be!" cried the outraged gentleman. "So do not think I am like to cry off."

"Before anyone says or does something which cannot be withdrawn," Lady Glendarvon interrupted, "allow me to point out that Glendarvon cannot be trusted near females. It is a well-known fact."

"Then it is time his lordship was taught it will not do," Sir Giles exclaimed.

"Sir Hedley, may I have a coze in private," Lady Glendarvon asked, and before he could refuse she had linked her arm into his and was leading him back towards the ballroom.

Left with the marquis Sir Giles said, "Dash it all, Glendarvon, this is too bad. My niece has a good deal to answer for, I fear."

"You heard what Lady Glendarvon had to say, Devine. Miss Westwood is not to blame in this matter. She was an unwilling party."

"I am not so sure of that. She comes from decidedly rackety stock."

Lord Glendarvon's manner gave way to a steely one. "Have a care what you say about a lady I deem to be incomparable."

Sir Giles stared at the marquis in astonishment for a moment or two before stepping back. "By gad, Glendarvon! Lady Devine will not credit this," he said before hurrying back to the ballroom and it was at this moment the marquis realised Amanda had gone.

Meanwhile Lady Glendarvon was saying to Sir Hedley, "I do hope you are being wise in calling Glendarvon out over Miss Westwood."

"It is a matter of honour, my lady."

"Naturally, and have no doubt I am fully in

favour of maintaining one's honour, but Glendarvon is such a crack shot. He cannot possibly miss. He never has before."

"Miss Westwood is worth the danger I shall be obliged to face on her behalf, ma'am."

"Ah yes, that is very gallant of you, Sir Hedley, but I do wonder if it is truly worth gambling with your life. She is without doubt the most entrancing creature, but since I have taken her up it has become more and more apparent that ... oh dear, I do hope this is not unkind but it seems Miss Westwood has an unfortunate addiction to ... gaming."

Understandably the young man appeared shocked and a little confused. "But, Lady Glendarvon ..."

"We have endeavoured to keep the matter a secret for her sake, redeeming vouchers and such, but you do see that I cannot in all conscience see you leg-shackled to that girl and certainly not fight a duel over her. A less worthy gentleman perhaps, even one possessing his own great fortune, but my regard and concern for you is of the highest, sir."

"Your concern is most welcome, my lady, but I cannot conceive how I did not know of this trait in Miss Westwood. I have not been far from her side at most social occasions."

"It is a family affliction I regret to say."

"I know she has been most concerned for Sir Cedric's gaming."

"She borrows from his meagre allowance to fuel her passion. Poor young man. He too covers for her. Her portion is large enough, I own, and will go to the man she marries, but he will be obliged to redeem all her debts which could be considerable."

"Lady Glendarvon," the young man said, looking ashen-faced, "although I shall continue to hold Miss Westwood in the highest esteem I am much obliged to you for your confidence. I had no notion she was so profligate. I am appalled that I almost called Lord Glendarvon out when he cannot be held to be to blame. Why did I not see her as the wanton she undoubtedly is?"

Lady Glendarvon smiled sweetly and patted him on the arm. "A handsome countenance is often a mask which hides a perverse nature. Now that is settled amicably let us return to the ballroom to enjoy what remains of the evening. I do see Miss Devine over there and I believe she is looking to be engaged by some young gentleman for the reel."

When Amanda reached the house she had called home for all those long weeks she contemplated packing her cloakbag and taking flight. Recalling her earlier attempt in similar circumstances she could not fancy that course. In any event there was nowhere for here to go and at that time of night flight would be sheer folly.

As she made her weary way up the stairs, nursing her aching heart, Lady Veronica came onto the landing to meet her. The girl was barefoot and in her nightshift and Amanda had never felt less like speaking to anyone let alone such an inquisitive child.

"Lady Veronica, what are you doing up and abroad at this time of the evening?"

"I was reading *The Terrors of Lucifer* and could not put it down even though I was obliged to keep all the candles burning in the room. Moreover I was in a fidge to see you."

"Well, if Miss Wheeler finds you out here, indeed awake, she will be as mad as a weaver."

The girl grinned. "Miss Wheeler is in Mrs. Dubbins' drawing-room, and they're both drinking porter. They do so every evening after I am put to bed although I am persuaded they believe no one knows about it." Amanda couldn't help but laugh and the girl went on. "In *The Terrors of Lucifer* I do think Miss Quiller would have far rather married Sir Lucifer than the handsome Mr. Colter. Do you not agree?"

"No, I do not," Amanda snapped and the girl looked at her curiously at last.

"I did not look to see you returned so soon. Is anything amiss?"

"I . . . was unwell."

"I do trust you won't be obliged to cry off any diversions, but I must confess you do look hag-ridden."

"That makes me feel so much better," Amanda answered in a weary voice. "Why are you waiting for me? Could it not wait until morning?"

"I was in a fidge to know if Sir Hedley came up to scratch."

Amanda's eyes opened wide. "Lady Veronica! What do you know about that?"

The girl looked self-satisfied. "I heard Mama and my brother talking of it yesterday."

"You should not eavesdrop, Lady Veronica. It is bad enough that the servants do," Amanda said in a severe tone and then, curiosity getting the better of her, "What did they say about the matter?"

Lady Veronica chuckled. "Are you certain propriety allows you to know what I heard by eavesdropping?"

"Oh, don't be so irritating, child," Amanda snapped.

"Mama told Fane she believed Sir Hedley was about to come up to scratch and he said . . ." she frowned with concentration much to Amanda's impatience, "Let me think of it exactly. He said if the pup was so insolent as to make an offer he would send him off with a flea in his ear!"

Amanda drew back, bridling with anger, "Did he, Miss Westwood?" the girl asked, her eyes wide with speculation. Amanda was fortunately saved the indignity of having to reply by the girl saying, "Oh, faddle. Here comes Fane. I had better be off or I'll be in for a real set-down."

She scampered up the stairs to her nursery. When Amanda glanced over the bannister rail it was to see the marquis striding into the hall. Without waiting to be seen she hurried to her own bedchamber where a maidservant dozed by the fire.

As the girl struggled to her feet, wearily Amanda dismissed her, wanting only to be alone. When the maid had gone Amanda made no attempt to prepare for bed. She felt utterly exhausted and sank down onto the sofa before the fire, but it would have been useless to go to bed for she knew she would not sleep. Peace of mind, it seemed, had gone for ever.

When there came a knock at the door she became tense but ignored it. However the maid had left the door unlocked and a moment later it opened and the marquis came in, displaying what was for him an uncharacteristic diffidence.

"May I speak with you for a few moments?"

Amanda stared into the flames of the fire. "There is nothing left to say."

Despite her discouragement he came into the room to stand by the fire in front of her. "You might want to know that Sir Hedley has withdrawn his offer of marriage."

"That does not surprise me."

"It does not seem to distress you."

"I only regret the outcome of tonight's fiasco. Sir Giles will tell Lady Devine what he saw and by the morrow news of my indelicate behaviour will be all over the Town. My reputation is in tatters. I don't suppose Sir Hedley is much in favour of defending my honour any longer, and I can only be glad of that. I want no blood shed on my account."

"You are uncommon in that, my dear. Most ladies feel honoured when gentlemen duel over them."

"I do not think you need to go so far. I have it in mind you will send away any suitor 'with a flea in his ear.' "

He looked startled at her terminology and then, recovering some of his urbanity confessed, "I am bound to admit that is true but only because I have found myself madly in love with you myself, Amanda, and would want you to be *my* bride." Amanda looked up at him at last and could discern nothing but sincerity in his demeanour. "Oh, I am fully aware you do not regard me highly and I cannot blame you for that," he went on. "You have good reason to be resentful of me. . . ."

She could listen to no more and jumped to her feet, her heart growing light. "Say no more, I beg of you! My heart was long ago lost to you!"

After staring at her in disbelief for a moment or two he drew her towards him once more, taking her into his arms, kissing her until she was breathless.

At last, when he drew away, he said, "Oh, Amanda, my dearest love, this will not do, not yet at any rate."

She blushed and averted her eyes, but he raised her chin so she was obliged to look at him again. "I do love you dearly."

Her eyes sparkled with happiness where, such a short time ago, there had been tears. "And I you. I never hoped to find such felicity."

He put his one free hand into his pocket and drew out a sheaf of papers. "Here, I have a wedding present for you. In all honesty I would have presented it to you, whoever you had chosen to wed."

"It looks to be an odd gift," she answered,

laughing. "In any event I have everything I want in you."

"Sincerely said and honestly meant, I do not doubt, but I am persuaded you will want this," he teased. "The title deeds to Westwood Hall." Amanda gasped and took the papers from him, looking at them in awe. "Back where it rightfully belongs."

After a moment Amanda looked at him again. "I am all but overcome by your generosity, my love. However, I am certain we shall not be able to spend much time there in the future. Lady Glendarvon speaks so fondly of Glendarvon Towers I cannot wait to go there as your wife."

"Then do tell me what you wish to do with Westwood Hall," he asked.

"Would you be very angry if I asked you to give it to my brother?"

As she looked up at him anxiously he smiled. "Amanda, I am so happy I would do anything you wished, but I deem it prudent to keep the deeds in my safekeeping until *he* chooses a bride." Contented she went back into the encircling comfort of his arms. "One thing I must ask of you. . . ."

"Anything, anything," she whispered, longing for his kiss.

"Do you plan for a literary future? If you do it is bound to come out that you are Emily Godrington."

Amanda couldn't help but laugh. "I think not. A future of married bliss, for that is what it will be, is not fertile ground for such tales."

His eyes grew suddenly dark. "It pains me to think you were in such agony, Amanda."

"It was all worthwhile if it has brought us together, for my happiness is all the sweeter. Does Lady Glendarvon know I am Emily Godrington?" she asked as his lips brushed the hands he held imprisoned in his own.

"I could not tell her until I was myself certain of it, and then only if you had sanctioned it."

"There will be two surprises for her when she returns," Amanda ventured, savouring the eventuality.

"Mayhap only the one. I fancy she will not be much surprised that I have declared myself."

She suddenly looked coy, glancing up at him through her lashes. "I had it in mind she expected you to offer for Mrs. Pettigrew."

He laughed at that suggestion. "Her ladyship knows me better than to think so." For a moment he appeared to be listening and then addressed himself to Amanda again. "I believe I hear Lady Glendarvon's arrival. We have but a minute or two before she arrives."

Breathlessly Amanda whispered, "Do not, I beg of you, let us waste a moment of that time."

He gathered her to him and began to kiss her again. For Amanda time stood still clasped in his arms and they were only vaguely aware that the marchioness had swept into the room.

After pausing in the doorway for a moment or two, she declared, "Did I not say you would make a brilliant match, my dear?" and then she hurried to give them her blessing.

Amanda could only anticipate the future with great joy and wondered what her friend Lucy would make of the situation when she wrote to tell her of it in due course.